# WRECK OF THE DAY

## A LOVE ME, I'M FAMOUS NOVEL

MICHELLE HERCULES

INFINITE SKY PUBLISHING

Paperback ISBN: 978-1-950991-25-9

# CHAPTER 1

## SAYLOR

The flight from Honolulu to L.A. is one of the hardest of my life. I keep my sunglasses on the entire time just in case I can't bear the pressure that's caving my chest in and I can't hold the tears back. I manage to keep my eyes dry, but barely. *Damn it*, I already miss him so much.

When the plane finally lands in sunny L.A., I have made another very important decision. If I'm going to depart from this world prematurely, I'm going to leave my mark on it, no matter what. Which means Wreck of the Day will no longer only be a garage band, even if I have to sell my soul to achieve that.

I grab a cab and pull my phone out of my purse to call Tabatha. It rings a couple of times before her sleepy voice comes through the speaker.

"Saylor?"

"Hey, Tabby. Did I catch you at a bad time?"

I hear the sound of sheets rubbing together. Tabatha is definitely in bed.

"No. What's up?"

"I'm on my way to your place."

"Wait? Aren't you supposed to be in Hawaii?"

"Change of plans. I caught an earlier flight. I really need to speak with you in person."

"Okay." Tabatha's tone of voice changes, mirroring my own. "Is everything okay, Blue?"

"Yes and no. I'll tell you once I get there."

I end the call and slouch against the seat of the car, letting my head fall backwards and closing my eyes for a brief moment. I feel my phone vibrate against my lap and my heart skips a beat. I fumble with the device, but when I don't see Oliver's name flashing on the screen, disappointment overflows my bruised heart.

The call comes from a private number, so I quickly reject it and look out the window. The afternoon sun is bright and annoying. I wish the weather was bad so it would match my mood.

On my way to Tabatha's, I get a text from Emma saying that she got all my stuff from my room. She doesn't mention Oliver. When I called from the airport in Honolulu asking her for the favor, I was adamant I didn't want to talk about him. She's respecting my wishes for now, but it will be a different story once she comes back into town. Emma doesn't know when to let a subject drop.

It takes over an hour to reach Tabatha's place in the busy L.A. traffic. In hindsight, I should have gone home first to freshen up, but I was afraid that if I postponed this conversation, I would chicken out. I pay the cab, get my suitcase, and I make a beeline to the side of the house where there is a small wooden gate. It opens to the path leading to Tabatha's apartment. Like me, she lives in the guesthouse behind the main structure.

I knock on the door, pushing it open when Tabatha tells me to come in. She's sprawled on the couch still wearing her PJs and watching something on TV. When I come closer, I see that one of the Harry Potter movies is on. It's the one with the guy from *Twilight*, but I can't remember the title for the life of me.

"Haven't you seen this movie before?"

Without glancing my way, she replies, "Yes. But I can't help it. Every time there's a marathon on TV, I have to watch it."

"But you own all the DVDs." I take a seat next to her.

"Not the same."

"So you like watching commercials."

Tabatha mutes the TV and turns to me. "You didn't catch an earlier flight back home just so you could give me shit about my weird habits. What's going on, Blue?"

I stand up, feeling nervous. I'm not sure where to begin, so I start with the easiest topic. "I want to give Wreck of the Day a real shot at something great."

Tabatha's eyebrows almost reach her hairline before she furrows them. "I thought that's what we had been doing for the past eight months."

"No. We were playing at being a band. We got lazy. We tolerated Damien for far too long. We were content to play at stupid frat parties."

"Those stupid frat parties helped pay the bills." Tabatha crosses her arms in front of her chest and flattens her lips.

"I'm not saying this to criticize your management skills, Tabby."

"Are you sure? That's what it sounds like, Saylor. What happened to you in Hawaii?"

I avoid her gaze and stare at the floor instead.

"This has to do with that manwhore popstar you were screwing, right? I saw the tabloid pictures of you two."

My gaze snaps up. "This has nothing to do with Oliver. I'm just sick and tired of being a garage band."

"Well, I'm sick and tired of that, too. But what do you want me to do?"

"We need to find a new drummer."

"No shit, Sherlock. While you were frolicking with your boy toy in paradise, Remi and I were busy looking for one."

"And did you find one?"

Tabatha shakes her head. "Not even close."

"Fuck! We need to find a new drummer." My sudden irritation comes out of nowhere and I bite my lip to keep from spewing more offhanded comments.

"I'm trying okay? What's the fucking hurry? I'm not going to just pick anyone this time. It's not like we have any gigs lined up. We have time to be more selective."

"No, we don't have any time!"

"What are you talking about? Don't tell me this *need* to make Wreck of the Day a hit A.S.A.P. is just so you can impress your new boyfriend. I thought you were bet—"

"I'm dying!" The words leave my mouth before I can stop them. I planned to tell Tabatha the truth but not like that. I take a seat on a chair nearby and put my head in my hands. "I'm fucking dying." My throat burns and at the same time, I feel hot tears stream down my face.

"What are you talking about?" Her voice comes out as a heavy exhale.

I take a couple of deep breaths and try to keep new tears from forming. Even so, my answer comes out choked. "I have a blood clot in my brain. I have an expiration date."

I keep my head down, but I hear Tabatha move closer right before she crouches in front of me. I glance up. Her face is a mask of coolness, but in the depths of her eyes, I see the shock she's trying to keep bottled in.

"Why didn't you tell me before?" A hint of betrayal manages to seep into her question and my heart clenches, hard.

"I-I couldn't."

Tabatha's jaw locks tight as her eyes narrow. "Is that why you were getting migraines?"

"Yes."

In a jerky movement, she stands up, and begins to pace. "Did you talk to another doctor? There must be something you can do. I mean, they could take the clot out. Did he say you couldn't have surgery, because I call bullshit on that."

"Tabby, stop. The doctor offered me that route. I refused."

She spins around and pins me with the mother of all glares. "You *refused*? Are you out of your God damned mind? You have to operate."

"No. I don't."

"Why not?"

"Because there are too many risks and I don't want to turn into a vegetable. I'd rather die."

"No. I won't accept that." Tabatha gestures with her hands, giving more emphasis to her words.

"You have to. We've made a deal." I lock gazes with her until she gets the meaning of my words. Her expression changes from pissed off to stunned in a split second.

"You can't be serious."

"Of course I'm serious. Seven years ago, before your heart transplant, you asked me to turn off the machines if you went onto life support because you knew your parents wouldn't have the guts to do it themselves. You asked me to basically help you die and I agreed. Now it's my turn."

Tabatha stares at me without blinking. I don't think she's even breathing. A minute passes by, but it feels like an eternity. She doesn't say a word before she breaches the gap between us and engulfs me into a tight embrace.

"Why, Blue? Why?"

"You know why."

I hear a sniffle and my vision becomes blurry. Here come the water works again. I pull back and see that Tabatha's gaze is bright. She's on the verge of losing it like me. She doesn't cry though. She holds it together because she's a warrior. She doesn't show weakness. She's fucking Ripley.

"Are you sure that's what you want? What do Liv and Mandy have to say about this?"

I walk away and turn my back to her. "I haven't told them. Actually, you are the only one who knows."

"Why do I have the feeling you aren't planning on telling anyone?"

I look over my shoulder and give her a rueful smile. "Would you do it if you were in my place?"

Tabatha takes a deep breath before replying, "No, I wouldn't." She runs a nervous hand through her ebony hair. "How long do you have? Did the doctor say?"

"A year at least," I lie. The doctor said I had from a month to a year, but I won't voice that out loud. I refuse to acknowledge I might only have one more month to live. No, if I believe I have a year, I'll get a year.

"Fuck. A year? That's nothing."

"Great things can be accomplished in a year, Tabby. If I'm being kicked out of this plane, I want to go out with a bang."

"With Wreck of the Day."

"Yes."

Tabatha's face breaks into a toothy grin, even if her eyes are still sad. "Nothing like a death sentence to motivate our asses. We're making Wreck of the Day the biggest fucking band that ever was."

"But we need a drummer."

"And she will be the luckiest woman on the planet because we are gonna rock." Tabatha raises her hand for a high five and even though she doesn't say it with words, I know we are sealing our pact. She will take my secret to the grave.

# CHAPTER 2
## OLIVER

## A WEEK LATER

stare at the TV but see nothing. I feel nothing, not even the cool rim of the vodka bottle on my lips, or the usual burning sensation as the clear liquid drains down my throat. I'm exactly at the point I wanted to be when I started my binge earlier. Numb. My eyelids are heavy and I let them drop, surrendering with pleasure to the reprieve only deep slumber can provide.

♡ ♡ ♡

*he sliver of sunshine poking through the blinds is what awakens me. I blink my eyes open and rub them for good measure, just in case my mind is playing tricks on me. I push the covers out of the way and jump out of bed, reaching my window faster than Harry can say hot chocolate, his favorite drink in the whole wide world. I part the heavy curtains and stare at the bright blue sky.*

*"Yes!" I say before I quickly change clothes and run out the door.*

*I fly down the stairs and I'm two steps away from the front door* and freedom when my father's booming voice calls my name from the dining room. Bugger. And here I thought I could escape unseen.

I trudge back and find Dr. Frank Best, sitting at the head of the long table with his face behind the newspaper.

"Sit down and eat your breakfast, Oliver."

Against my will, I do as he says without a peep. I can't risk him grounding me today of all days, when the sun has finally decided to make an appearance after an entire week of stupid rain. Mrs. Connelly appears a second later with a plate of beans, eggs, and sausage. She pours me a glass of milk and leaves the room as quickly as she can. No one likes to linger too long in my father's presence. He's a beast.

I'm almost done eating when Harry comes in, his brown hair sticking out in all directions, and still wearing his PJs. Without a word, he takes his seat, and like magic, Mrs. Connelly reappears and puts a full plate in front of him as well. I don't know how she knows exactly when we need something.

"Where are Mother and Charlotte?" I ask.

"Out." Dad doesn't glance up from his reading.

"Louis and Eddie invited me to go fishing today," I say.

"Really? Can I come?" Harry asks, his eyebrows almost reaching his hairline.

I'm about to say 'no' when my father cuts in. "Of course you can join your brother. I'll have Lawrence drive you after breakfast."

Bloody hell. I can't do anything without Harry tagging along.

Twenty minutes later, our driver Lawrence drops us off at the Larrington's stately home. The white building looks more like a fairy tale castle than anything else. My mother says it's disgustingly beautiful. I don't know what she means by that. How can something disgusting be beautiful?

My friend Louis meets us outside. "Couldn't get rid of the baby, huh?" He nods in Harry's direction.

"No, Dad made me bring him. Where's Eddie?"

Louis moves closer and whispers in my ear. "He's by the lake, on the lookout."

"Lookout for what?"

*"You'll see. But we'll have to get rid of your brother." Louis turns to Harry who is busy throwing rocks up in the air.*

*It's embarrassing that I have to bring him with me everywhere I go. Louis is right. He's a baby. No ten-year-old should be forced to hang out with his six-year-old brother.*

*"Hey, Harry. Do you like hot chocolate?" Louis asks.*

*"Yeah."*

*"Go on inside then. Our cook just made some."*

*Harry dashes into the house, no questions asked. That was easy.*

*"Come quickly." Louis motions for me to follow him. We take the path that leads to the property's lake.*

*"What's going on?"*

*"My cousin Lucy and her uni friends are spending the weekend with us. They like to swim in the lake," Louis pauses for effect before continuing, "naked."*

*"No way."*

*"Way."*

*Ten minutes later we find Eddie, Louis's older brother, hiding behind some bushes by the edge of the lake. We crouch next to him.*

*"Any tits yet?" Louis asks.*

*"Not yet, they just got here."*

*We only have to wait a few more minutes before Lucy and her friends get ready to remove their clothes. My heartbeat accelerates. I've never seen a naked girl before, at least not in the flesh. Lucy takes her bikini top off and we're about to be rewarded with a spectacular view when Harry comes running in our direction, shouting my name at the top of his lungs. The girls scream and put their clothes back on as soon as they discover our hiding spot. There goes our chance.*

*Harry stops in front of us, his face covered in chocolate, and something inside me snaps.*

*"You idiot! Look at what you've done."*

*Harry's eyes turn as round as saucers and I can see he's about to cry. With trembling lips, he asks, "What did I do?"*

*"You ruined everything. Like always. Go away, you stupid brat."*

*Harry turns on his heel and runs back to the house, wailing. It doesn't take long for me to feel like dog shite. I'm a terrible brother.*

*"I hope Lucy doesn't rat us out," Louis says.*

*"I should go check on Harry."*

*"He'll be fine," Eddie says. "Come on, let's go fishing."*

*I hesitate for a split second before I follow Eddie and Louis to the dock. Great dark clouds form in the sky and the light breeze changes.*

*"I think a storm is coming," I say but my voice is swallowed up by the howling wind.*

*Suddenly, Louis and Eddie vanish and I'm surrounded by black smoke. I feel dizzy and disoriented before the darkness clears and I find myself back at home. I'm in the entrance foyer and from there I can hear loud sobs coming from the living room. I follow the noise and when I enter the room, I see my mother sitting on a chair, crying non-stop, while two men wearing police uniforms talk to my father. They notice my presence, and when Dad's gaze collides with mine I know something terrible has happened.*

*"Where's Harry?"*

*Mum cries harder and Dad ignores me, turning back to the police officers. I ask again and again where Harry is, each time my voice growing more desperate, but no one pays any attention to me. Finally, Mrs. Connelly pulls me to the side and answers me.*

*"Dear boy, Harry is dead."*

♡ ♡ ♡

My eyes fly open and I sit up in my bed. My skin is clammy and my heart is going two hundred miles a minute. *What. The. Fuck.* I thought I was over this shit. I hadn't dreamt about my brother in years. I get out of bed and notice the empty bottle of vodka on the floor. No wonder my head is pounding like a motherfucker. Even so, I make a beeline for the wet bar in the living room, break the seal of a brand new bottle, and pour myself a generous dose. I drink it like it's water, but the spirit does nothing to dissipate the dream or the nauseating feeling it brought forth.

I reach for my phone on the counter and pause when I realize what I'm doing. My finger is hovering over Saylor's name. It's been a week since she left me in that hotel room in Hawaii. A week without hearing her sexy voice, without seeing her beautiful face. A week of hating her and going back to loving her in the span of seconds. It has been a struggle keeping my distance from her. The craving hasn't stopped. It will never stop.

I give in and press the call button. It rings and rings while my heart gets stuck in my throat, while my lungs can't draw in air. She doesn't answer. Deep down I knew she wouldn't. What happens next is worse. I get her voicemail instead. I get to hear the raspy voice that drives me insane, asking me to leave a message. I don't. What would be the fucking point? I don't have a game plan yet.

A second later, the phone vibrates in my hand but it's not Saylor's name flashing on the screen. It's my sister's. I should answer it. I've been blowing her off for weeks now. I just stare at the device as if I'm in a trance. When I come to it, the call has already gone to voicemail. *Shit.*

Charlotte's usually cheery voice is stern. She wants me to attend the charity ball our parents are organizing. Mum has been on my case for months, pestering me to confirm my presence. If she's using Charlotte as a last resort, she must really want me there. I could blow her off like I've done countless times before, but I could use a break from California. Plus, if I want to enlist Charlotte's help to get Saylor back, I better plead my case in person.

I call my travel agent as I walk back to my room. I want to be on the first flight out to London.

$\heartsuit \heartsuit \heartsuit$

have not shaved in a week, so all I have to do to conceal my appearance is to wear a baseball cap and sunglasses as I power walk through LAX airport. I barely had time to shower and pack before I had to be at the airport. By the time I finally reach the gate, everyone is already boarded. One quick look at the sour puss expression of the check-in woman tells me she's not happy I'm late.

"Sorry, luv. Traffic was brutal." I smile and I get nothing, not even a hint of recognition.

"Have a nice flight," she replies tersely after she scans my phone.

Okay, then. I hope her mood is not a preview of what my trip will be like. Once inside the aircraft, the flight attendant is much more pleasant, but that's because I'm flying first class and she has no choice in the matter. I remove my sunglasses and hat as I walk to my window seat. A mop of ginger hair catches my eye and as I sit down, I recognize the guy.

Allan Eriksson, the most down to earth heir to a billion-dollar fortune I've ever met, is sitting next to me across the aisle. His father might own this very airline company. I can't remember exactly. He has his head down, scrolling through his phone.

"I didn't realize I was flying with royalty tonight," I say.

My comment draws his attention and he looks up.

"I'll be damned. Oliver Best, what are you doing here?"

"Flying back home to attend a stuffy charity ball my parents are organizing. You?"

He shrugs and puts his phone away. "Getting away from my mother."

I laugh. Allan's mother is something else. A gazillion times worse than mine. She's a country music legend and one could say if Nashville had a court, she would be queen.

"I'm honored to be flying with the prince of Nashville."

He frowns. "Don't call me that."

I shake my head. "How's that gig at ET Online working out for you?"

The last time I met Allan for drinks he told me he had gotten a job working behind the scenes on the TV show. It was an entry level job, pretty much a glorified slave position he was able to secure without his mother's help.

"It's been brutal, but I'm learning a lot. I got promoted to assistant producer."

Allan's answer makes something click in my head. I don't know why I've never considered the idea before, but it's fucking brilliant.

"Mate, no offense, but you look haggard. I bet they are working you to the bone. I understand the need to not depend on your family's money, but you are wasting away in that job."

"Jeez, thanks a lot. What do you want me to do, ask Mommy Dearest to help me find a better job? Believe me, she has offered, several times. I don't want to ride on her coattails."

I grin from ear to ear. "I have a better idea. Come work with me. I'm starting a music production company. I'm looking for a partner. You would be perfect."

Allan watches me through slits. "Why? Because of my mother's connections?"

"No. Because you are a decent guy who doesn't get on my nerves."

My answer seems to surprise him. He keeps staring at me as if he wants to read my mind.

"I don't have any money," he finally says. "I only have access to my trust fund when I turn twenty-five."

"Money is not a problem. You come in with the work. Something tells me you are way better at running the day-to-day operations than me."

He shakes his head and smiles. "That sounds too good to be true. What's the catch?"

I hadn't thought of a caveat, but now that Allan posed the question, I do have a challenge for him.

"No catch, but a task. I'll give you partnership if you sign a band I've had my eyes on for a long time."

"That's it? You want me to sign a band? That sounds too easy."

I laugh. "Mate, you are in for a treat. Only one condition, though. Stay away from the lead singer."

"Why?"

"Because she's mine."

# CHAPTER 3
## SAYLOR

When we told Remi that we wanted to take Wreck of the Day to the next level, starting off by finding a kickass female drummer, she was totally onboard. And when we went to Closing Time to ask for Rori's help, Remi was prepared to offer the guy free meals at the Goulas for life. It didn't come to that. Rori was more than happy to help us. He even had the brilliant idea to hold open auditions at his pub, making an event out of it.

Today is audition day and Closing Time is packed, more crowded than usual for a Saturday night. I don't know what magic trick Rori pulled, but we have people bursting out of the seams and the best part of it, plenty of talent to sift through.

Unfortunately, no one qualified enough has performed yet and I'm beginning to lose motivation. Either the girls are good but don't have the right vibe, or they aren't good at all. My head is beginning to pound and I don't think my condition is to blame. I rest my forehead in my hand and sigh loudly when the last unfit contender exits the stage.

"Maybe you should let guys audition," Remi says.

"Hell no. I won't have another dick pissing all over our band," Tabatha replies.

"Tabby is right. If we don't find the right person tonight, we'll keep looking." I sit up straighter in my chair.

*You could also call him,* a pesky voice in my head says. Oliver did offer to help me find a new drummer. It's not only pride that's keeping me from taking him up on his offer. It's also fear. Fear I won't be able to hide my feelings from him. Fear I won't be able to push him away.

Rori hops onto the stage and announces we have time for one more audition before Oreo's band kicks off tonight's entertainment. Right now, only Oreo himself is on stage, playing the guitar to accompany the drums. Tabatha leans back on her chair and takes the shot of tequila we just ordered.

Remi looks around, searching the crowd. She sits up straighter and announces, "Oh, that girl has potential."

Tabatha and I look in the direction Remi's gaze is trained on, and we see a young woman wearing a tank top, boyfriend-style jeans, and carrying drumsticks. Her face is hidden under the baseball cap she wears.

"How can you tell? We can't even see her face," Tabatha asks.

Remi turns to Tabatha. "I don't know. A hunch?"

"Well, your hunch might be completely wrong, because the girl just bailed," I say as I witness the chick turn on her heel and bolt out of Closing Time.

"What? No way." Remi jumps out of her chair and starts for the door. "I'll be right back."

Tabatha and I trade glances. "What is she going to do? Drag the girl back in by her hair?"

I shrug. "It's possible. You know when Remi gets one of those hunches, she can't be dissuaded."

Ten minutes later, Remi comes back in with the runaway drummer in tow. I'll be damned. Remi is good. I hope she's not wrong about this chick. She looks like a scared mouse right now with the way her gaze is glued to the floor and how she's holding her drumsticks as if they were her lifeline.

On the stage, she exchanges a few words with Oreo and

seems uncomfortable to be there. I shouldn't fault the girl for being shy. This is a large crowd and everyone will be judging her. She takes her place behind the drums, but I'm surprised when Remi goes behind the keyboards.

"What's Remi doing?" Tabatha frowns.

We don't have to wait long before the first notes of Nerf Herder's theme song for *Buffy* fill the room and runaway girl does her thing. I glance at Tabatha and her expression is priceless. She's the biggest *Buffy* fan there ever was and it's easy to see she's pleased with the girl's music choice.

I close my eyes to properly evaluate her skills. I separate the guitar notes from the melody so I can dissect every beat of the drums. The song lasts two minutes or so, but it's enough to tell me the last contender is the best we've seen tonight. The crowd seems to agree by the way they cheer on her performance. Maybe Remi's intuition was dead on. But we won't know for sure if she's a fit before we talk to her.

Remi brings the brunette to our table like a proud mama bear.

"Ladies, meet Elisa Gutierrez. This is Tabatha, and Saylor."

"Hi, Elisa. Nice to meet you. You were really good out there," I say.

"Thanks. You can call me Sticks."

"Oh, I like that nickname." Remi pulls up a chair. "Come, sit with us."

"Okay." Sticks puts her drumsticks on the table and I notice the quote tattooed on her wrist. *"This too shall pass."* She catches my stare and pulls her hand from the table, placing it on her lap and out of sight.

"So, where are you from, Sticks?" I ask.

"I'm originally from a small town in Colorado. I moved here a few months ago."

"How old are you?" Tabatha cuts in a little too harshly, earning a glare from Remi.

"Uh, I'm nineteen. Is that a problem?"

"No, of course not," Remi replies. "I'm twenty. Tabatha and Saylor are twenty-two. So, do you go to college?"

Sticks looks down at her hands. "No, I took a year off. I plan to start community college next year."

"Is going to college something that's important to you?" I ask.

She raises her head and looks me in the eye. "Shouldn't it be?"

"Yes. Of course, but what I want to know is what's your biggest dream, a college degree or playing the drums? There's no wrong answer here but everyone at this table is one hundred percent committed to the band. We can only bring someone on who's on the same page as us."

"If I had to pick, I would choose the drums. Music is the only thing that—" She pauses abruptly and looks down again. "It's the only thing that makes my heart sing."

I'm satisfied with Sticks' answer and by looking at the rest of the band, I see they share my sentiment.

"Alright. We would like to give this a try, Sticks. Come to my place tomorrow for practice and we'll go from there," Tabatha says in a much friendlier tone.

"Really?" The girl perks up on her seat.

"It's a trial period, of course. We need to jam together to make sure you are a good fit for us."

"Yes, I totally understand. Thank you so much for the chance."

Excitement shines in Sticks' eyes, illuminating her face and changing her completely. We all carry demons, but the one-eighty shift in Sticks' demeanor reveals perhaps her inner battles are as fierce as mine. No matter what problems she has, she's here, pursuing her dreams just like me and that makes me like her even more.

# CHAPTER 4
## OLIVER

stop in front of the luxurious Hollingsworth Hotel and it's déjà vu. I haven't been here since Sebastian's surprise birthday party organized by his girlfriend at the time, Gretchen. So much has happened since then.

The valet opens my door and I hand him my car keys, making sure to add fifty quid to that as well. I don't need to say a word. The bloke knows he needs to take special care of my Aston Martin. I hadn't realized how much I missed my car until I slid into its plush interior earlier. I'll have to bring it back with me when I return to California. Sure, it would be easier to just buy another one there, but this particular car is special, it represents my declaration of independence.

As I walk through the hallway of the pretentious hotel, I notice how many women turn their heads to have a better look at me. *Yes, ladies, it's Oliver Best. Former member of Boys Future and forever a sex god.* Too bad for them I'm off the market. There's only one woman I want.

A man wearing a tux greets me at the double doors and asks for my name. I want to laugh, but instead I just raise an eyebrow at him.

"The name is Best, Oliver Best."

Sure, I pulled a James Bond move, but I couldn't resist. Upon hearing my family's name, the poor sod turns whiter than the tux shirt I'm wearing.

"Of course, sir. Welcome."

I walk in and stop for a moment to get a feel of the room. Upon a quick scan, I see nothing has changed. The same arrogant, highly elite people my parents love to mingle with are here. Those closest to the door turn to look in my direction. I bet my chosen profession is fodder for endless gossip among those vultures, much to my mother's detriment.

I spot her sitting at the best table right in the middle of the great ballroom, surrounded by her closest friends. Even with the distance, I notice the hard set of her shoulders and the unhappy expression on her face. She turns to my sister, angling her body over the empty chair between them, to whisper in her ear. It's a question Charlotte responds to with a shrug. I'd bet a million pounds Mum is asking her where the hell I am. I'm late and dinner service has already begun. I move in their direction and pull out the empty seat next to Mum's. She glances in my direction with a frown.

"Where have you been, Oliver? You are late," she asks under her breath. She can't chide me too loudly in front of her friends. What would they say?

"I lost track of time."

"Right," Charlotte mumbles.

"Hello, sis." I raise the champagne glass in front of me in salutation before drinking the whole thing in one big gulp.

"Your mother tells me you're planning another trip to Africa," one of the women at the table addresses my sister. "Is Joseph accompanying you?"

"Joseph?" Charlotte snorts before composing herself. "No, he will not."

"Who the hell is Joseph?" I frown at her.

Everyone at the table glares at me. The woman who asked

the question answers with an air of disdain. "Joseph Whitman the Third, of course."

I give her a blank stare. Am I supposed to know who this bloke is? If I have to judge by his last name, he's a pompous ass, member of a pretentious family.

I turn to Charlotte. "I didn't know you had a boyfriend."

"And are you surprised about that?"

I don't miss the jab. After what happened to Harry, I tried my best to push everyone away. I took for granted Charlotte would always be there for me when I needed her, no matter how badly I treated her. Maybe she finally got tired of her arsehole brother.

I pull at my tie, feeling suffocated by the constraint around my neck. Not even ten minutes into this dinner from hell, I'm already jonesing for something stronger than alcohol. A waiter places a plate of salad in front of me, but I can't eat anything right now. I stand up suddenly and all eyes are on me again.

"Where are you going?" my mother asks through clenched teeth.

"I need to make a call."

I move away from the table without bothering to wait for her reply. Funny how Dad is nowhere in sight. I bet he came up with a last minute excuse to skip this nonsense. I swear this is the last charity event my mother will rope me into. Not even a week back in London and I can't wait to leave this dreadful town.

The problem is not London or even Mum. The problem is I'm miles away from the woman I love without any idea of how I'm going to win her back. If I knew why she left me alone in that hotel room in Hawaii in the first place it would help a lot. If Saylor had told me she didn't care for me, I could learn to accept it. But I know that's not the case. Deep in my bones I know she has fallen as hard as I have.

I make a beeline to the nearest bar and order a double dose of whisky. With the drink in hand, I place a call to Allan. It's noon in Los Angeles, so he should be working already. He answers on the third ring.

"Hey, Ollie. What's up?"

"I want to know if you've made progress with the task I gave you."

"I got back in town a day ago."

Not the answer I wanted to hear. I take a large sip of my drink. "So, you don't want the partnership."

"You know bloody well that is not the case. As a matter of fact, they are playing at a popular venue in L.A. tonight and I plan to approach them after the show."

"Fine. But remember, don't breathe a word that I'm involved with the company."

"Sweet baby Jesus. What did you do to this woman that she can't know you own the company that wants to sign her band?"

"Nothing. She's stubborn and proud. She won't sign with Renegades Productions if she knows I'm behind it."

Allan is silent for a moment before continuing. "I can relate to that. But even so, it's misleading as hell."

"If that's going to be a problem for your southern morals, I'll look for another partner."

Irritation simmers low in my gut. I don't know what's going on with Allan. He didn't seem to have a problem keeping my name out of the negotiations when we discussed the details of his mission before.

"I'll do it. I just don't think that's the best approach to win your girl back."

He is fucking right. Saylor is going to have a cow when she finds out she signed a contract with my company. But she won't do it if she knows I'm involved, and I honestly want to help her succeed. She has real talent, but the music industry is rough. I don't see a problem with me giving her the initial push.

"Don't give yourself premature stress lines over that. Just get them to sign the contract."

"Okay. You got it, boss."

Allan ends the call before I can reply. If it had been any other person, I would be fucking pissed. I've known the guy for a while now and his attitude and moral compass will be good to balance things out. I need someone at the helm of the company who is level headed and can make sound decisions, who is also not afraid to go against me. But he'd better not screw things up with Saylor tonight otherwise I'll have to make his life hell.

# CHAPTER 5
## SAYLOR

"Let's take a break." I remove my strapped guitar and place it on the stand next to the amps.

"We haven't nailed the new song yet. We sound awful," Tabatha argues.

"And we're not going to sound any better if we keep playing non-stop. I need food." I keep on walking until I'm out of Tabatha's parents garage where we now practice every day for five hours at a time.

I inhale the end-of-summer crispy air and stare at the bright sky. Footsteps follow me and I know without glancing over my shoulder that it is Tabatha.

"The gig tonight is a big deal, Blue. Many music producers are known to scope new talent at Ray's Venue."

"I know." I can feel Tabatha's scrutinizing stare burning a hole through my face. "My head is fine, so stop staring at me like that."

"Just checking."

I turn to her. "I haven't had a migraine episode since I came back from Hawaii."

Tabatha narrows her eyes at me and crosses her arms in front of her chest. "You'd better be telling the truth, Saylor."

"If I knew you would become a pain in my ass, I wouldn't have told you anything." My tone is light and Tabatha smirks at me.

"When was I not a pain in your ass?"

"True that." I let out a sigh. "I know tonight is a big deal. I want to nail that new song as much as you do. But don't forget Sticks has only been with us for less than a week. She's not used to our intense jam sessions yet."

Tabatha's shoulders sag as she exhales. "You're right. It's just…" she pauses and looks into my eyes. "I have this feeling, Blue. Somehow, I know tonight is our night."

"Oh, not you now with the feelings and premonitions. I thought only Remi suffered from those."

"Suffered from what?" the girl in question asks as she joins us.

"Tabatha has a *feeling* about tonight."

"You too?" Remi's eyebrows shoot to the heavens.

A shiver runs down my spine. I don't think Remi is joking about that. My stomach turns into a ball of knots as anxiety takes hold. I can't let jitters run rampant through my body. We must nail the new song more than ever. I need a distraction, so I turn to Tabatha.

"How about we go scavenge your mom's kitchen for some grub, Tabby? We need full bellies if we're going to keep practicing until perfection."

A smile blossoms on Tabatha's face. "She made Cuban sandwiches for us."

My stomach grumbles just at the thought. "Lead the way."

I follow Tabatha back inside, but even the prospect of delicious food can't take my mind off of what's going to happen tonight.

♡ ♡ ♡

peer at the crowd from backstage and the butterflies in my belly become radioactive. This is the biggest crowd Wreck of the Day ever performed to. And we are singing a bunch of our own songs tonight. We usually do covers because that's what the college scene demands. But we need to sing original songs if we want to impress label scouts, so the stakes are much higher.

I head back to where the girls are chilling out. Tabatha is pacing across the room with hands clasped behind her back and her gaze down. It's her ritual. Sticks is sitting on the beat up couch, twirling her drumsticks up in the air. Her beautiful dark hair is in a ponytail and her face is hiding under a baseball cap. I'm beginning to think that's her signature look. Remi is next to Sticks, devouring a double cheeseburger bigger than her face. I don't know how she maintains her slim figure with the amount of junk food she puts into her body.

Tabatha senses my approach and stops to look at me. "How is it?"

"Full house."

She nods once and resumes pacing. I let her be and walk toward Remi and Sticks. It will be Sticks' debut show and I want to make sure she's okay. I sit on the couch's arm next to her. "Nervous?"

She stops twirling her sticks to glance up at me. "No. Should I be?"

I don't detect an ounce of bullshit in her relaxed demeanor. The girl is as cool as a cucumber. What a difference from when she auditioned for us a week ago.

A wiry man with spiked hair and more piercings on his face than Pinhead appears in my line of vision. He introduced himself earlier but I can't, for the life of me, remember his name. My brain immediately latched on to the *Hellraiser* reference and that was the end of it. He's the assistant manager of Ray's Venue.

"Are you ready to go on?"

"Yup." I turn to Sticks and Remi. "Chicas?"

Sticks just nods and Remi wipes her face with a napkin before answering with her mouth half-full. "Swuure."

Ten minutes later, we take our places on the darkened stage and wait for our introduction. Someone in the crowd yells 'Break a leg, Blue' and I suspect Levi is behind it. I hope Remi manages to keep her cool. Her secret crush on the surfer boy can get the better of her sometimes.

The previous loud rumble from the audience lowers to an expectant murmur. When the stage lights turn on, I forget the nervousness and let the music take over. The exhilarating feeling is like a drug to me and I will never get tired of it.

After the first song, I know we have won the audience, and the show keeps getting better and better. We are rocking this place. I barely notice the passage of time, and before I know it, it's over. Tabatha's and Remi's intuitions were right. This is by far the best show we ever put out since Wreck of the Day was formed. We are finally in sync.

When we exit the stage, we are laughing and talking animatedly, still high from a perfect performance.

"Oh my God. That was awesome!" Remi shouts.

"Yes, it really was."

We all turn to see who the owner of that voice is. An attractive ginger guy is looking at us with a smile. His hands are tucked inside his jeans pockets in a casual way, but the messenger bag he carries makes me think he is not at Ray's Venue for pleasure.

"Thanks. And you are?" I say.

"I'm sorry. That was rude of me. My name is Allan Eriksson. I'm from Renegades Productions."

"Renegades Productions? That name doesn't ring a bell." Remi angles her head as if it will help her decipher the guy.

"I've never heard of them," Tabatha adds in her usual blunt way.

"No, you wouldn't. We're a new music production company,

looking to sign our first band. I really liked what I saw out there and I would love to chat a little bit with you."

Remi steps closer to the guy, narrowing her eyes in the process. "You look familiar."

Allan seems surprised by her comment. "I do?"

"You are Sharona Westwood's son," Sticks says, earning Allan's attention.

"Wait? The Queen of Nashville Sharona?" I ask.

He hesitates before saying, "Yes."

Holy shit. The son of a music legend liked our show. Not only that, but he's from a music production company. I usually take Remi's *feelings* with a grain of salt, but what if she had been right? She glances at me with a sparkle of excitement in her eyes.

Tabatha raises her hands and shakes her head. "Stop and back up. Are you the owner of this new production company or is your mother behind it?"

"My mother has nothing to do with it and yes, I own it."

Tabatha glances at me and I nod. He sounds legit. "Alright. Then let's chat, Allan Eriksson," she says.

We head to one of the offices at the back of Ray's Venue, which turns out to be a small meeting room. I'm trying my best to control the accelerated beating of my heart. I can't believe a production company wants to talk to us. Okay, an unknown company, but still, it's hard not to get excited.

We take seats around the oval table and are soon enveloped by a heavy silence. We are all waiting for Allan to start talking, but the dude is now looking at Sticks intently. I can't tell if he's attracted to her or not. He's definitely an unreadable person.

"So…," I say.

He blinks a couple of times and looks in my direction. "Right. Sorry, I'm a bit in awe. You guys were fantastic out there. Blew my socks off."

I trade a glance with Remi. She's fighting hard to keep the giggles bottled in. Who talks like that? His southern accent makes it even more amusing.

"Thanks," Tabatha replies.

Allan notices Remi's reaction and his face turns a bright shade of red. "Sorry. I tend to talk like my grandfather when I get excited."

"Could you tell us a bit more about your company?" I say, trying to steer the conversation back to business.

"Sure. Like I said earlier, we're a new music production company and we're looking to sign our first band. We don't want to take on more than four artists or bands a year. That's how we differentiate ourselves from our competitors. We feel working with just a small group of talented individuals will allow us to really tap into their potential."

"You don't even have a website," Tabatha says while she's looking at her phone. "How do we know you're legit?"

"We didn't get around to building a website yet."

"Facebook page?" she continues.

"Nope."

"How *new* is your company exactly?" She leans forward and watches the guy through slits.

Allan's face turns red again. "A week old."

Tabatha and I look at each other. She's not happy about that and the truth is, Allan's admission makes my enthusiasm dial down a notch as well.

"I know it doesn't sound good and I would have first taken care of the basic details like setting up a website etcetera, before approaching any talent. Unfortunately, my partner was adamant that I come check you out tonight."

"Oh, I didn't realize you had partner," I say.

"Yes, I have a silent partner."

"That doesn't sound like a silent partner to me," Tabatha says and Remi glares at her.

I don't know why Tabatha keeps antagonizing Allan. Who cares if he has an investor? Most companies have several.

Allan seems to be at loss for words for a moment. "Well, he used to be in the business before, so he has suggestions."

"What do you mean by that? Was he a musician? A producer?" I ask, unable to hide my curiosity.

Allan shifts on his chair as if my question makes him uncomfortable.

"He used to be in a band," he finally confesses.

"Don't leave us hanging like that. Who is he?" Remi leans forward, eager to know who the mysterious investor is. I guess at this point, we all are.

"Well, I'm not at liberty to disclose that information."

"Why not?" Tabatha asks, and Allan turns in her direction.

"Because they are going to build up mystery and momentum surrounding his identity, and only make a big revelation when the time is right," Sticks answers before Allan can, earning a smile from him.

I'm amazed as well. It sounds like Sticks' has some background in marketing, which is always a plus.

"Exactly," Allan continues. "He also doesn't want to influence anyone because of his high profile. But let me assure you, if you sign with us, you'll be in excellent hands."

"You want to sign us?" Tabatha sits up straighter in her chair.

My heart jams against my ribcage and my legs begins to bounce under the table.

"Absolutely." Allan pulls a stack of papers from his messenger bag. "I had a feeling that tonight I would find our first talent." His voice is earnest and sincere. He pauses briefly and looks down at the papers in his hands. "This is usually not how things work, but I brought a sample of the contract we are prepared to offer you." He slides it over to Tabatha who quickly scans through the document.

"Like I said, that's a sample contract. Your final contract would be more specific. I can forward it to your manager."

"I'm the manager," Tabatha replies without taking her eyes off the papers in her hands.

"Oh, okay then. Here's my cell phone number." Allan stands

up and distributes his business cards to everyone. "Call me when you're ready."

"I gotta go," Sticks announces suddenly.

"Really? I was hoping we could grab some drinks." Allan sounds disappointed.

I wouldn't mind having drinks with Allan if only to get to know him better. But Tabatha shakes her head and says, "I would like to read this contract carefully first."

"Sure thing. I'll look forward to your call."

♡ ♡ ♡

During the ride back to Littleton, we can't stop talking about Allan and his proposal. Well, everyone is chatting excitedly besides Sticks, who just remains quiet looking out the window. I haven't been able to figure her out yet.

When we pass the Welcome to Littleton sign, Tabatha asks if she should drop Sticks home first. We are all going back to Tabatha's to pour through every single line of the sample contract.

"If you don't mind. I'm beat. You can fill me in on your decision tomorrow," she says.

"It's your decision too, Sticks. You are part of the band now." Remi twists in the front seat, a frown on her face.

Sticks removes her baseball cap and runs a nervous hand through her hair, messing up her ponytail in the process. "This is happening so fast."

"And it's all because of you. You are our lucky charm." Remi smiles.

"I hope I don't disappoint," she mumbles so low, I can barely hear it.

"So, home or my place?" Tabatha probes again.

"Your place."

Tabatha's parents' suburban, two-story house is Wreck of the Day's headquarters. Her parents support her dreams one hundred percent and go out of their way to accommodate the band's needs. Mr. Larouche, Tabatha's father, even gave up his two-car garage and soundproofed the space, giving the band a permanent place to practice.

Getting detention in junior high was the best thing that happened to me that year. It was when I met Tabatha. She was an angry teen back then, dealing with her own demons, just like I was, and we totally clicked. But instead of getting into more trouble than we could handle, we turned our angst into music.

The light on the porch is the only source of illumination, the rest of the house is shrouded in darkness. It's already past three in the morning, so no surprise there. We stopped at an In and Out on the way home, eliminating the need to scavenge the fridge in the main house. Instead, we trudge to the back of the house to Tabatha's place.

The décor is nothing you would expect from Tabatha if you were to judge by her clothing choices. The place is minimalist to the point of being painfully bare, with white walls and white furniture, and only a few splashes of black here and there. The furniture aesthetics emulates the sixties, and anyone who knows Tabatha well, will immediately get the *2001: A Space Odyssey* reference.

Remi places the takeout bags on the round table facing the kitchen and we all sit down.

"Shall I read the contract out loud?" Tabatha asks.

"You better," Remi replies. "I don't know why Allan didn't give us four copies."

"Maybe he's environmentally conscious." I smirk at her and she rolls her eyes.

It takes twenty minutes to read through the entire document, and Tabatha highlights the parts we have questions about. It all sounds too good to be true. The sample contract even gives the advance amount and that alone would mean I could buy a more reliable car.

"What do you guys think?" Tabatha asks.

"Too good to be true?" Sticks voices what I was thinking a minute ago.

"Ugh, guys. Why the negativity? This is the opportunity of a life time," Remi replies.

"I'm not so sure, Remi. The company doesn't have a website or any social media presence. I'm not saying they have bad intentions, but how do they plan to promote us when nobody knows who they are?" Tabatha points out.

"What about the silent partner? Allan said he used to be in the biz. Plus, Allan himself comes from music royalty," I say and Tabatha frowns at me. We are usually on the same page when it comes to this type of thing.

"Don't count on him using his mother's fame in our favor. He has nothing to do with her," Sticks says.

We all look in her direction but it is Remi who poses the question, "How do you know so much about him?"

Sticks glances down and clenches her jaw. She doesn't answer Remi's question right away which to me speaks volumes. After a moment, she finally raises her head and lock eyes with Remi. "His mother owns a mansion in White Peaks and my mother used to work for her."

"So, you know Allan?" I ask.

Sticks shakes her head. "No. I don't know him. But tonight was not the first time we were in the same room together."

"Oh, shit. He didn't even recognize you. What a jerk." Remi crosses her arms and frowns.

"He wouldn't. I've changed a lot since the last time he saw me."

"Do you think he can be trusted?" It's Tabatha's turn to ask.

"Honestly, I don't know."

"Okay. Here is what I propose we do. Dad has a good friend who is a lawyer. I'm sure he won't mind looking over the contract for free," Tabatha says.

"Sounds like a plan." I stretch my arms, finally feeling the effects of a very intense week. My body is about to crash. I stand up, ready to say goodbye, when Tabatha speaks again.

"I know I'm the minority here, but I want to know who the silent partner of Renegades Productions is before we sign anything."

Not knowing the identity of the investor is not a deal breaker for me and I'm sure Remi shares my sentiment. Sticks, I don't know. The hard set of Tabatha's jaw and her squared shoulder tells me this is not a fight we are going to win tonight.

# CHAPTER 6
## OLIVER

run across the expanse of my living room, wrapped in a towel, as I search for my phone. I don't know why I didn't bring the sucker with me into the bathroom. I'm expecting a call from Allan and this better be it. He was supposed to call me about Wreck of the Day first thing in the morning, but it's already eleven a.m. in California. Anticipation is killing me. I was never a patient person. The phone stops ringing before I can locate the damn thing. Fuck!

I find the device under my couch and see I missed Allan's call. I don't bother listening to the voicemail message he left and call him right back. He answers on the first ring.

"Oliver, I just—"

"Did they sign it?" I cut him off.

"I guess you didn't listen to my message. They sent the contract over to a lawyer, but their manager was adamant about one thing."

"What?"

"They won't sign until they meet you."

"How was my involvement even brought into the conversation?" I ask through clenched teeth. Allan was supposed to say he owned the company solo.

"They found it strange that our company had no online presence and I let it slip the reason I went to see them prematurely was because my silent partner insisted."

*Son of a bitch.*

"Damn it, Allan. Saylor won't sign the contract if she knows I'm behind Renegades."

"Don't worry. I created the mess. I'll fix it."

I want to believe in Allan's confident tone, but I don't see how he plans on doing that. Unless he's thinking about using his mother's influence somehow.

"Care to share?"

"Not yet. When are you getting back?"

"I'm catching a flight tomorrow."

"Good. I'll see you tomorrow then."

I end the call and stare at nothing. If Allan fails on his mission, I'll need a backup plan to convince Saylor to sign with us. The bass player is the manager, Saylor told me that. I don't think she likes me very much. I look down at my phone and scroll through my contacts until I find my sister's number. The fact that she's not saved to my favorites says a lot about our relationship.

The phone rings and rings and I'm certain she will let the call go to voicemail. I'm prepared to keep calling until she answers. It doesn't come to that. Her annoyed voice comes through the speaker.

"What do you want, Oliver?"

"Hey, Char. Catch you at a bad time?"

"Yes, I was watching *The Office*, it's the *Gossip* episode."

"Wait, were you watching *The Office* with Steve Carell?" I've seen a snippet of it on Facebook, that's how I know. I haven't watched either version.

"Yes, duh."

"Traitor."

"Whatever. So, what do you want?"

"I'm flying back to Cali tomorrow and I was wondering if you are free to have dinner with me tonight."

"A bit late for a dinner invitation, don't you think? I already ate and I don't feel like going out anyway."

"Fine. Can I come over then?"

There's a pause and I can practically hear the gears in my sister's pretty head working. She knows I'm up to something.

"It depends. Are you drunk? High?"

"No. Jesus, Charlotte."

I begin to pace and regret calling my dear sister.

"What? You can't blame me for asking. Fine, you can come over. But you'd better bring ice cream. I don't have any left."

She ends the call before I have the chance to reply.

Twenty minutes later, I'm knocking on my sister's apartment door in Chelsea, one of the trendiest neighborhoods in London. She's been living on her own since she was eighteen. I'm not one bit surprised that she managed to convince our overbearing mother to let her live by herself in the city. Growing up, Charlotte was a manipulative brat. She always got what she wanted by only batting her eyelashes and saying exactly what Mum wanted to hear. Since I never had the stomach for ass kissing, sneaking around my parents was my MO. Charlotte was the perfect daughter and I was the rascal, the black sheep. Whatever.

She tells me to come in.

"Why is your door unlocked? It's not safe." I walk in and find her on the couch.

"Oh, you want to play the concerned brother now?"

I bite my tongue. I deserve every snarky remark Charlotte throws at me. I'm a shitty brother, always have been. She's still watching TV, all rolled up in her blanket like a human burrito, and doesn't spare me a glance as I walk to the kitchen to grab a couple of spoons.

Her decoration screams wealth and by the combination of modern and classic, I know Mother didn't have a say in here. It's all bright and clean. I remove my shoes before stepping foot in the living room, because Charlotte will have a fit if I stain her white fluffy rug.

I put the ice cream container on her coffee table, and sit on the small space next to her. I make a motion to dive into the creamy dessert, but Charlotte snatches the container, keeping it out of my reach.

"Who says you can have any?"

"I bought it. Are you going to eat all that? Your ass is going to double in size. What will Joseph Whitman, the Third say?"

"I don't fucking care what he'll say. He's not my boyfriend anymore."

I raise an eyebrow at her. "Oh?"

She rolls her eyes and looks at me. "He cheated on me, okay? Besides, he was a bore."

"I thought you liked the pasty, insipid types."

"No, Mum likes them. I just follow along. It's the path of least resistance."

I narrow my eyes at her. "Right, because getting the golden star for being the perfect daughter doesn't suit you at all."

She shrugs and smirks at me. "Unlike you, dear brother, I don't make millions by singing a bunch of idiotic songs to a bunch of idiotic girls."

"Someone is not bitter."

"Whatever. Enough about me. Please state the reason of your visit and leave."

She's not joking, so I don't beat around the bush. "I need your help with a girl."

Charlotte freezes mid-motion, the ice cream spoon half way to her mouth, and drops her jaw. "Excuse me?"

"Please, don't make me repeat it."

She places the spoon back into the ice cream container and stares at me without blinking. Then she throws her head back and laughs. For a whole minute. When she finally has the giggles under control, tears have streamed down her cheeks.

"I'm glad that I amuse you," I say through clenched teeth. I knew coming here would mean giving Charlotte enough ammunition to tease me for a lifetime. Yet, here I am, because Saylor is worth the humiliation and much more.

"Oliver Best has found a woman he can't woo on his own? Next, you're going to tell me you are in luuve." She bats her eyelashes and places a hand over her chest.

When I don't say anything, I expect the hysterics to restart. Instead, Charlotte just watches me in silence with her big hazel eyes.

"I'll be damned," she finally says. "You *are* in love. Oh my God. I can't wait to meet this girl."

"And you will. If you agree to help me."

I see when Charlotte becomes excited with the idea, but the upturn of her lips tells me her help comes with a price.

"I'll do it under one condition. You must help me convince Mum and Dad to let me transfer to DuBose College."

I frown at her. "What about Oxford?"

She avoids my gaze and stares at the TV. "I never wanted to go there."

I'm not sure if I believe Charlotte or not. We were never close. Oxford has my parents' hands all over it, so it's possible she truly doesn't want to attend the prestigious institution. In reality, I don't care what she does with her life, but the fact she wants to give Mum and Dad the middle finger suits me well.

"My sweet sister, it will be my pleasure."

# CHAPTER 7
## SAYLOR

We meet Allan in a trendy restaurant in Manhattan Beach, just outside of L.A., two days after Ray's Venue concert. When we arrive at the location, he's already waiting for us. A bolt of apprehension ties my stomach into knots. This is happening so fast. Are we making a mistake? I don't have the time to recover from one.

Allan's ginger hair is styled perfectly with just a hint of hair product in it. His jaw is framed by strawberry blond scruff which does nothing to make him look older. He stands up as soon as he sees us come into the restaurant, and I notice his *Highlander* T-shirt, 'There can be only one'. My worries lessen a fraction, at least he has good taste. Mom's love for the hit 80s movie rubbed off on me.

"Ladies. A pleasure meeting you again."

We shake hands and then Allan asks us to take a seat. My gaze skates around the restaurant before I look straight into his eyes. "Is your partner coming?"

Not that it's a big deal to me, but if it will make Tabatha happy, I'm all for it.

"Uh, my partner?"

"Sure. You don't expect us to sign a contract without at least meeting the not-so-silent partner, do you?" Tabatha raises an eyebrow at him.

"He's not ready to announce he's part of Renegades Productions yet. It's all part of our marketing strategy as I said before."

"What? You don't think we can keep a secret?" Sticks asks a little too harshly.

"That's not it." He frowns and stares at her intently. "You look familiar. Have we met before?"

Remi opens her mouth, but Sticks flashes her with a pleading gaze, making Remi swallow her response.

"No," Sticks says.

I elbow Tabatha to catch her attention. She leans closer and I whisper in her ear. "What are we going to do if he insists on not giving the name of his partner?"

I have a known expiration date. What if Allan takes away his offer and we never receive another? What if this is our only chance to get out of obscurity? The lawyer said the contract is solid. Who cares who the silent partner is, really?

I don't get to hear Tabatha's answer because Allan continues to talk and diverts my attention.

"I have news that will hopefully make you believe our company is one hundred percent invested into turning Wreck of the Day in one of the most successful bands in the world. We've lined up Scott Rowan to record a song with you."

There's a minute of silence at the table as each of us processes what Allan just said. My head is spinning. Scott freaking Rowan.

Remi is the one who recovers first. "The country music legend?"

Allan's grin spreads from ear to ear. He knows he has us. "The one and only."

I'm as shocked as everyone else. Scott Rowan is one of the most successful country singers in the nation. At twenty-eight years old, the guy has had more number one hits than Lionel Ritchie. He's the male version of Taylor Swift.

"We're not a country band," Tabatha says.

"He wants to branch out."

I peer at the girls and all of them but Sticks seem won over by the prospect of recording with Scott Rowan. With her face partially hidden by her baseball cap, it's hard to read her expression. However, the thin flat line of her lips tells me she's not as enthusiastic as the rest of us.

Tabatha glances at Allan again. "If we sign the contract, there must be a clause in it about the collaboration with Scott Rowan. I won't take your word for it."

Her response shocks the hell out of Remi if I'm to judge by how her eyebrows almost meet her hairline.

Allan doesn't seem offended by it. He actually smiles before replying, "Naturally. So, can I put the champagne order in?"

We all turn to Tabatha and with a big smile, she replies, "Hell yeah."

# CHAPTER 8
## OLIVER

"Cheers, mate." I raise the cold beer bottle in my hand before taking a long sip of the dark liquid. I grimace when the bitter taste hits the back of my throat—I was never a fan of the beverage—but I can't afford to partake in my usual fare of hard booze. I need to stay sharp if I want Renegades Productions to succeed.

I'm back in L.A., busy as fuck getting my company off the ground. It was a premature move to sign Wreck of the Day before we had all our ducks in a row, no doubt about it. For that reason, Allan and I have been working around the clock and such distraction has kept me from obsessing too much about Saylor. But one can only work so much non-stop before collapsing. So I called Bas—fresh from his honeymoon—to join me for a beer.

"Cheers," he replies and takes a sip of his drink as well.

I lean back and take in my surroundings. I found this gem while strolling in the middle of the night, getting acquainted with my neighborhood. Hermosa Beach isn't lacking in cool little restaurants and this one in particular has a killer fish taco on their menu.

"How was your trip to London? Did you like being back there?" Bas asks.

"Are you mental? I had to deal with my parents and piss poor weather. I'm glad to be back here."

Bas shifts on his chair and avoids my gaze. He seems uncomfortable and I know why. Saylor running away soon after his wedding without saying goodbye didn't go unnoticed. At least, no one thought I had done something awful to make her bail like that.

"Alright, let's cut the bullshit. Just ask me about Saylor already."

"What happened, mate?"

I run a hand through my hair and look at my beer glass. "I don't have a bloody clue. Maybe it was too much, too fast. Saylor couldn't handle it."

Bas shakes his head and takes another sip of his beer. "That's fucked up. I was rooting for you two."

"Don't worry. It's temporary."

My statement makes my friend narrow his eyes at me. "Ollie, what are you planning?"

"Remember when I told you I wanted to start a music production company?"

"Yes. Renegades Productions."

"Well, we just signed Wreck of the Day."

My mate stares at me with unblinking eyes for a minute, frozen. "You signed Saylor's band? I can't believe she would agree to that."

My lips unfurl into a smile. "She doesn't know I own it. I made Allan partner and he's the one dealing with them."

"Oh, fuck. That's how you plan to get Saylor back? You're crazy if you think that's going to help. She'll be furious."

"Probably."

"You have to tell her."

"Not yet. Charlotte thinks I should wait."

Bas raises both hands up. "Wait. Charlotte is involved? How the fuck did that happen? You don't even like your sister."

I shrug. "Desperate times require desperate measures. I needed a female perspective and Charlotte is the best I've got. She flew in today actually and she's already driving me insane. And it's not like I can come to Liv for help."

Bas shakes his head again. "Whatever. It's your grave."

I roll my eyes. "Please. I may be whipped, but I haven't lost my game yet."

I'm done talking about Saylor. It's time for a change of subject. "So, do you plan to go back to school?"

"Yeah, eventually." He shifts his gaze down and curls both hands around his pint. I've known my friend for far too long to be able to detect the subtle change in his body language.

"Cut the bullshit. What's eating you?"

"Nothing. I like going to college. It's the people that can be a bit problematic."

"Ah, I see. You thought you could just go back to being a regular Joe."

"Yeah. Wishful thinking, I guess. I've been out of the lime-light for over a year now, but I still get stopped by fans. People still make jokes at my expense. I'm relieved that I took a semester off."

"Then don't go back. You have plenty of money. Fuck, join me at Renegades. It will be epic."

"I have to go back. It's what my parents always wanted for me, to graduate from a good school, to find a job I loved, to lead a fulfilling life."

"Okay, I just vomited in my mouth hearing you spill those bull-shit Hallmark movie lines. I hate to break it to you, mate, but your folks are dead. Sticking to a path you're not passionate about just to fulfill their wishes is fucking nuts. Do what makes *you* happy."

"You're an ass."

"I know."

We don't say anything for the next couple of minutes. I'm giving Bas time to mull over my words. I would understand dealing with the harassment at college if a degree was something he truly wanted. Doing it to please people who are long dead is mental. He's the one who re-initiates the conversation.

"Tell me a bit more about Renegades."

*A-ha.* That's the Bas I know. My mood shifts at once and I tell him everything about the company. Who we've lined up to work with the band, our plans to launch their first single, and so on.

"I'm thinking about asking Zawe to help with the band's video." I lean back and wait for Sebastian's reaction with a smirk. Our old choreographer used to give him hell.

His eyes widen before he bursts out laughing. "Oh my God. Please let me be there when Zawe whips Saylor's ass into shape."

"You can if you are part of Renegades."

His smile fades a bit, turning into a small grin. "I need to speak with Liv first. That's a big decision to make."

"Sure, mate."

We are laughing about a stupid joke when I feel a presence looming behind me. Bas glances up and immediately frowns. I turn around and come face to face with Craig Hawthorne, one of the sleaziest gossip reporters I ever had the displeasure of crossing paths with. Last year, after Sebastian's departure from Boys Future, the arsehole started making insinuations and spreading lies about my friend and me. When he got into my face while I was out clubbing in London, I lost my cool and introduced him to my knuckles. He tried to sue me, but thanks to my family's connections, the assault charges against me were dismissed and to boot, Craig also lost his job. Needless to say, he hates my guts now.

"My my, look what we have here. A Boys Future reunion, I see," he says with a smirk and my hands curl into fists.

"Piss off, Hawthorne," I say.

"When my sources told me you were moving to the US, I couldn't believe it."

"Well, believe it. Now run along before I call security."

Craig narrows his eyes and clenches his jaw.

"Don't mess with me, boy. You're far away from your family's influence, and daddy won't be able to bail you out of trouble when you screw up again."

"Jesus, I think I just pissed in my pants. That's how terrifying you are, Craig."

Sebastian laughs, earning him a glare from the man.

"Go ahead. Make childish jokes all you want. We'll see who will be laughing in the end."

"Say, Craig, did they teach you those cliché villain-esque lines at the shitty school you went to, or were you just born lame?" I say.

The balding, short man turns red and that makes my amusement grow. I wish he would lose his shit in public. Too bad he doesn't. He turns on his heel and stomps away. Good, my knuckles were itching to connect with his jaw again.

"Do you think Hawthorne will create problems for you?" Bas still staring at Craig's retreating figure.

"Oh, I'm sure he will try, but he'll fail again."

# CHAPTER 9
## SAYLOR

We're warming up for practice at Wreck of the Day's official headquarters—A.K.A. Tabatha's parents' garage—when Remi comes running in, holding a *Rolling Stone* magazine in her hands. She trips over my purse's strap on the floor and dives head first into the bean bag in the corner. It would have been comical if weren't for the stricken look on her face when she flips around.

"Whoa. Where's the fire?" I help her get up.

She pushes the hair out of her face and shoves the magazine into my hands. "You need to read this."

Tabatha and Sticks come closer, making a circle around me. "Read what?" I ask.

"I marked the page."

I find the folded page corner and right in the middle of the magazine, there's an article on one side and the other is a full page picture of Oliver. I stop breathing for a moment. It hasn't been that long since Hawaii, but looking at his crooked smile, even the two dimensional version, feels like a sucker punch to my guts.

I force my eyes to peel away from his face and read the article. It's an interview with him. Honestly, I'm just scanning the words, my brain seems to have gotten frozen as well, until a name pops up on the page—Renegades Productions. I read the phrase twice and then I look up.

"He owns the company?"

"What's going on? Tabatha pulls the magazine from my hands.

"Oliver Best is the silent partner!" Remi shouts and I wince.

Tabatha mutters a curse and shakes his head. "That's why the cloak and dagger attitude from Allan. Son of a bitch. We've just been duped."

Sticks's gaze bounces around our group. "I don't understand. What's wrong with this guy? Didn't he used to be in a boy band? He probably has connections."

Tabatha crosses her arms in front of her chest and glares in my direction. "I'll let Saylor answer that."

"We dated. Briefly." I don't want to get into too many details. It was bad enough lying to Remi about why I wasn't with Oliver anymore. She had been certain we were meant to be together.

"And?" Sticks continues.

"Saylor dumped his ass but the idiot is just crazy enough to come up with a fake production company just so he can wiggle his way back into her life," Tabatha answers for me.

Remi whips her face toward her. "He wouldn't do that. Come on. That's nuts."

I raise both hands up. "Stop! We're not going to solve anything by throwing random theories left and right." I grab my purse from the floor.

"Where are you going?" Remi asks.

"To get answers."

♡ ♡ ♡

'm not angry at Oliver. I'm furious to the point I can't see straight. But I still manage to drive from Tabatha's place to his house in Hermosa Beach without causing an accident. He'd better be there because I feel like murdering someone.

I can't believe he tricked me like that. He knew I wouldn't have signed with Renegades if I'd known he was behind it. What does he think he will accomplish with that? My eternal gratitude? Me forever eating from the palm of his hand?

Fury is the only thing keeping me from succumbing to the ache in my chest. To work with him, even in a limited capacity, will be agony. He's everything I never knew I needed. But he can't ever know that.

I park in front of his house and march up the front steps. I press the doorbell and won't let it up until someone answers the door. I hear footsteps approaching and I prepare myself to come face to face with the man I can't forget. Only, it's not Oliver who answers the door, but a gorgeous brunette wearing nothing but a guy's button down shirt.

I'm frozen, my tongue is thick in my mouth, but my heart is thundering inside my ribcage.

"What the bloody hell are you doing?" The girl glares at me. She can't be older than eighteen.

I also notice the British accent. I knew Oliver had gone back home after Hawaii, Liv told me. So it seems he brought someone back with him. My stomach bottoms out and I think I'm going to be sick. I curl my hands into fists and dig my nails into the softness of my palms. The pain doesn't do anything to help. On the contrary, dark spots appear in my line of vision and I sway on the spot. *No.* I cannot have a fainting episode now, not in front of Oliver's latest conquest.

"Shit. Are you going to throw up?" She looks over her shoulder. "Oliver!"

I close my eyes and place the heel of my hand against my forehead, not that it does any good. Before I open them again, a strong arm wraps around my shoulder and his sexy voice reaches my ear. "Saylor, sugar. Are you okay?"

I want to push him away but I have no strength left. I feel drained and his body flush against mine is not helping one bit. I look up and my gaze connects with his beautiful eyes. I had forgotten the impact they have on me. So, so dangerous.

Oliver seems concerned and I find myself melting into his embrace, until I remember the half naked woman still staring at us. My spine goes taut and I take a wobbly step to the side.

"I'm fine. I need to speak to you."

I walk in without being invited, shoving the brunette out of my way. She lets out a yell of complaint but I don't look back as I walk up the stairs, holding the rail tight to avoid falling flat on my face. That would ruin my performance. Even though I'm in shambles inside, I can't let them see it.

I don't know what I expected to find in Oliver's living room, but it's definitely not start-up central. The couch, chairs, and coffee table are gone and have been replaced by office furniture. There's a massive whiteboard hanging from the wall where a modern painting used to be. The only thing remaining from before is the flat TV screen.

What catches my attention is the big sign with Renegades Productions logo propped up against the wall. I'm angry all over again. I pivot on the spot when I feel them behind me.

"I take it you've read the article," Oliver says.

"Yes, asshole. That was a low move, even for you."

The girl chuckles as she walks to the open kitchen so I turn my ire on her. "What are you laughing at? Shouldn't you be on your merry way out the door or are you waiting for payment?"

Oliver's eyebrows shoot to the heavens, before a grin appears on his stupid face. The girl looks at me like I've lost my mind, then she turns to Oliver. "She has no idea who I am, does she?"

The infuriating man has the audacity to shrug. "Nope. Never saw a reason to mention you to her."

"Ouch. That hurt, bro." She puts a hand over her heart, faking being upset.

"Okay, what the hell is going on here?" I put my hands on my hips. It seems I'm the only one not in on the joke and I hate the feeling.

The pretty brunette walks over to me and extends her hand. "Hello, I'm Charlotte Best, Oliver's sister. Nice to meet you, Saylor."

My jaw drops and I turn to Oliver, ignoring Charlotte's hand. "You have a sister and it never occurred to you to tell me?"

"I thought you knew."

I throw my hands up in the air. "Why would I know that?"

"Because Ollie is a self-absorbed prick and he thinks everyone is obsessed with him," Charlotte answers before pulling up a chair to sit down.

"Bugger off, Charlotte. Go put some clothes on. Allan will be here any minute," Oliver says without taking his eyes off of me.

"Fine. I'll leave you two love birds alone."

She jumps off the chair and disappears down the hallway, leaving me alone with Oliver. Now I wish she would come back because I don't know how to act around him. My heart is screaming at me to jump into his arms while my head is saying no. That's an unfair battle with the way he's staring at me like he wants to devour me. How can my brain remain in control? Shit, it must remain in control. Besides, I'm supposed to be furious at him, not get all hot and bothered.

"Are you feeling better? Would you like to sit down?" he asks.

"Cut the crap, Oliver. Why did you sign Wreck of the Day? Is this some kind of sick joke or is it punishment because I left you?"

He raises his hands up. "Whoa. Slow down. I signed Wreck of the Day because you guys are good. Please don't mix things up here. This is a strictly professional relationship."

I cross my arms in front of my chest and narrow my eyes.

"Right. And you want me to believe that. Then why did you keep your identity a secret until we signed the contract?"

"Would you have signed it if you knew I was involved?" He raises an eyebrow.

"Hell no."

"You have your answer."

"That's manipulation and such a dick move."

Oliver walks to the wet bar—surprise, surprise it's still there—and pours himself a drink.

"I don't know why you're so upset. You should be thankful I don't hold grudges. You did leave me alone in that hotel room without so much as a note of goodbye. Who's the dick now?" He turns to me and smiles, only there is no amusement in his eyes. He's hurt. Shit, I did that.

"I'm sorry."

He clenches his jaw before draining his drink. "No worries, luv. I'm resilient. I'll survive."

He moves closer and I fight the urge to run away. He doesn't invade my space as I expected he would. Instead, he offers me his hand. "Let's let bygones be bygones, shall we?"

I stare at his hand—a hand that has caressed every part of my body and gave me more orgasms than I can keep count of—for far too long before I shake it. The contact only lasts a split second before he lets go and walks to a desk, taking a seat behind it. His face is cold, all business like. I should be happy Oliver doesn't have ulterior motives here, that all he wants is a business relationship with me, but my heart doesn't want to accept that. It cracks open, it bleeds, it dies.

"Are you working on any new songs?"

"Yes." My reply comes out as a croak and I have to clear my throat before continuing. "A few."

"Good. And do you still practice in Tabatha's garage?"

"Yes."

Oliver nods and glances at his computer. "I would like you to move your practices here."

"What?"

"I bought this big ass house with the intent to make it the Renegades headquarters. I turned the basement into a kickass music studio. It has everything you will need, including top of the line instruments."

I put my hands on my hips. "We have instruments already."

"I know, but I think you will like your new ones." He doesn't smile but there's a twinkle in his eyes that had been missing before.

"I have to talk with the girls."

"Sure thing. I can show it to you now if you'd like."

The idea of going down to a basement alone with Oliver terrifies me, so I shake my head. "Another time. I have to get back to Littleton."

"So, are we cool?"

No. We're the opposite of cool. But I can't say that. I should be glad Oliver has accepted what we had has ended even if a huge part of me is disappointed he has given up so easily.

"Yes, of course."

♡ ♡ ♡

## OLIVER

I wait until Saylor leaves to grab the bottle of whiskey and pour myself another generous dose. I'm already on my third glass when Charlotte waltzes back into the living room.

"Wow. That was intense."

"Shut up, Char."

"I hope all those drinks you're inhaling are because you are celebrating."

"Celebrating what?"

"Oh, brother mine. Saylor is totally into you. She almost bit my head off because she thought I was one of your conquests."

"Her little act of jealousy means nothing."

Charlotte comes closer and swats the back of my head.

"Ouch! What the fuck was that for?"

"You are Oliver fucking Best. Stop acting like the *Deathly Hallows Part One* Ron."

I glower at her, but Charlotte just laughs. "I gotta say. It's freaking awesome to see you so whipped."

"I'm glad I amuse you."

"So, what's your master plan? Since you were able to keep your cool and not attack the woman, I assume you're going to take my advice."

"Oh, to play the aloof, hard to get guy? It's all so childish." I fill my glass again.

"Yes, it's childish indeed. You could just sit down and talk like adults. What's keeping you from asking Saylor why she left you without an explanation after the *amazing* week you spent in Hawaii?"

I don't miss the sarcastic tone in Charlotte's voice and I flip her off. She rolls her eyes.

"Because she'll give me a bullshit excuse. She's hiding something and the only way to find out is by keeping her close."

"You know you sound completely mental, right?"

"Wait until you fall in love, dear sister."

"Nope. I'll pass."

I take another sip of my drink. "I said the same thing not too long ago."

# CHAPTER 10

## SAYLOR

"What's up with you, Blue? You're quieter than normal," Tabatha asks as we wait in a big board-room in the five-star hotel Oliver stayed at before. We're finally meeting with the rest of Renegades Productions team, but for some reason, he didn't want to meet at his house.

"Nothing, I just want to get this meeting over with."

As soon as the words leave my mouth Allan comes in, followed by a man and a woman we've never met before. No sign of Oliver. My heart clenches as a myriad of emotions crashes inside. I feel like a stupid high school kid, in love with the unattainable popular jock. Only I'm the one who threw my chance at love away. Getting over him feels like an impossible task now.

"Sorry for the delay. I got stuck in traffic." Allan sits down without making eye contact with any of us. "This is Teresa Wallace, and Garin Burton."

We all wait for Allan to add on to that, but he seems flustered and oblivious to our confusion. He was the one who scheduled the meeting in the first place, but he was also pretty vague about it. He just said we would discuss Wreck of the Day's marketing plan, whatever that meant.

Garin and Teresa stare at Allan for a moment, before Garin turns to us. "Well, I'm Garin Burton, Marketing and PR consultant and this is Teresa Wallace, ow—"

"I can speak for myself, Garin," Teresa cuts him off. "I'm Teresa Wallace, owner and CEO of Stellar Image Consulting."

The job title drips from her mouth like she just announced she's the freaking queen of England. Her long, shiny ebony hair doesn't have a strand out of place. Her pale face is covered with heavy make-up, a vain attempt to hide the fine lines on the sides of her mouth and forehead. Her dark gaze roams over each of us, scrutinizing and calculating. Sudden annoyance sours my mood. I glare at Allan, willing him to look up from his phone to see how pissed off I am. There's nothing wrong with our look to warrant an image consultant.

Silence prevails until Garin turns to Allan. "Um, do you want me to start?"

Allan finally glances up, but he still seems distracted. "What? Yeah, sure."

I don't like one bit his obvious lack of interest in this meeting. I hope he's just having a bad day and he will get over it soon enough. Garin fires up his computer and a PowerPoint presentation appears on the big white wall at the end of the long table. I turn my attention to what the short man is saying, ignoring the feeling of discomfort in my belly.

After an hour of Garin talking about the launch of Wreck of the Day, he turns the floor to Teresa. She opens a leather-covered notebook and addresses all of us.

"Before I even start talking about my plans for the band's image, let me make something very clear. You all need a makeover."

The hairs on the back of my neck bristle, and I prepare for a fight, but Tabatha speaks first.

"The hell we do."

Tabatha's outburst is loud enough to wake up Allan from whatever far away land he had been for the past hour. He sits straighter on his chair while Teresa raises a perfectly plucked eyebrow at Tabatha.

"Are you gay?" she asks.

"Excuse me?" Tabatha narrows her eyes.

"Are you a lesbian? Do you like to eat pussy?" Teresa continues nonplused.

Tabatha is one second from launching herself across the table and tackling the annoying bitch to the ground.

"Tabatha doesn't fancy chicks, not that that's any of your business," I say.

"Oh, it *is* my business. Everything you do is my business. I'm not a glorified stylist. I own one of the best image consulting companies in the country. My job is to make sure your image sells music. That includes not only clothing and hair style, but positioning, who you are associated with, etc. Show business is all about perception. Tabatha's clothes and hairstyle are screaming lesbian at me. It would be fine if she were, but since she isn't according to you, I don't want to give your future fans the wrong idea."

"I'm not gay," Tabatha says through clenched teeth.

"Then we need to change your look. There's nothing to be done about your hair length. It's too short and extensions would look ridiculous. You'll have to let it grow out. But we can definitely do something about your clothes."

Tabatha looks down at her patchwork dress. "What's wrong with my clothes?"

"The question is what isn't wrong with them." Teresa turns her attention to Sticks who as usual, is hiding under a baseball cap. "You, Sticks, right? Could you please remove your hat? I can't see your face."

Sticks does as Teresa asks, obviously not wanting to cause more drama. Her brown hair is pulled back in a pony tail and her face is devoid of any make-up. Her warm olive skin is flawless. I'm not the only one in the room staring at Sticks. Garin can't hide his admiration, whereas Allan is looking at Sticks through slits, as if he's trying to place her. I can't believe he has not recognized her yet.

"Oh my God, what's wrong with you?" Teresa bursts out, and Sticks becomes smaller in her seat. "And here I thought I had to call my plastic surgeon. Why in the world would you hide your face under that ugly hat?"

"I, uh…" Sticks sputters.

"No more baseball caps for you. I want the world to see you."

Sticks glances at me in panic. It's as if the hat is not a mere accessory, but a shield. Maybe Sticks is hiding from the world.

"The baseball cap is her signature look. She's gonna keep it," I say.

"Absolutely not! Over my dead body," Teresa shouts.

"Then you'd better start organizing your funeral." I stand up, ready to put an end to this idiotic meeting.

"She can keep the hat," Allan says and Teresa turns her murderous gaze in his direction.

"I won't have you question my judgment. I'm the best for a reason. If they won't follow what I say, then I'm afraid I can't work with them."

Allan takes a deep breath and leans his elbow on the table. "Fine. You can leave."

"What?" Bitch-face was obviously not expecting that. "Are you firing me?"

"Yup. Your services are no longer required."

The woman glares at everyone present before standing up with all the dignity she can muster. "That's what I get for agreeing to work for a bunch of amateurs."

"Bye, Felicia." Tabatha waves at her.

The air becomes lighter with Teresa gone, but not by much. I'm keen to start working on our single with Scott Rowan. Music is all that really matters to me and all this business and image nonsense has drained my energy. I need something positive to look forward to.

"So when can we expect to meet Scott?" I ask.

"Soon, I promise. He has a few commitments this month. Meanwhile, I've arranged a moving company to transfer your equipment to the studio in the headquarters. Oh, and we want to record your first single next week." Allan types something on his phone.

"I thought our first single was going to be with Scott," Remi says.

"No," Garin replies. "As I said in my presentation, it's best if your first single is not the collaboration. We want you to be already on the road to success when we release the single with Scott."

"Oh, I guess I spaced out for a moment."

"I didn't agree to the move. We're fine practicing at Tabatha's place." I cross my arms.

"Uh, no we are not." Remi turns to Tabatha. "No offense, Tabby, but that garage gets hot."

"I'm sure my folks will love to get their garage back." Tabatha throws me an apologetic glance.

I clench my jaw and glare at the glass of water in front of me. I guess this is a battle I can't win.

♡ ♡ ♡

After the meeting with Allan and Garin, I head to Liv's place. I haven't see her since the wedding, and I vowed to spend as much time as I can with the people I love.

She looks as radiant as I thought she would. Her happiness is like a beacon of light and she can't stop smiling. She tells me everything about her honeymoon, and I listen with a grin of my own, even if it's not as happy as hers. The ache in my chest is still too raw for that.

"Is it going to be hard working for Ollie, Blue?"

I shake my head. "I don't think so. He's been surprisingly

mature about it. We're maintaining a strict business relationship."

"That's not what I asked." Liv stares at me knowingly and I look away.

"It will be fine."

"I'll pretend I believe you. Now, let's talk about something else. I have a huge favor to ask you."

I turn to her again. The chipper tone of her voice makes me curious. "Okay?"

"You know that Reinhardt Corp. throws this huge charity gala every year, right?"

Reinhardt Corp. is where Liv has been working since she got fired from the Hollingsworth hotel—thanks to the Sebastian mess. It's owned by our friend Rodrigo's family, and even though he doesn't like to get involved in the hiring process, he was the one who referred Liv for the job.

"Yes, Rodrigo always complains he has to attend the party. He says it's super boring." I narrow my eyes at her. "How come I have the feeling I'm not going to like what you have to say?"

Liv bites her lip and glances down at her lap. "The band my boss hired for it cancelled yesterday. He called me, panicked, asking for my help, even though I'm still on vacation."

"What a jerk."

"No. That was awesome. It means he's relying on me more and more."

Liv looks so enthusiastic I don't have the heart to say her boss is being a huge prick and he's taking advantage of her.

"Anyway, I suggested Wreck of the Day." She peers at me through her thick eyelashes, her gaze expectant.

"Oh, Liv. The songs we play are not the kind those people expect."

She reaches out and touches my arm. "No. That's where you are wrong. We've decided to do something fun this year for a change. Wreck of the Day will be perfect. Please, Blue. Say you will talk to the girls. It would be mean so much to me."

"Oh, I'm sure they won't say no. But I have to check with Allan first. I don't know if we're still allowed to book our own gigs."

"If he makes a stink, I'll ask Oliver."

My spine goes rigid. "Please, don't. I'm sure Allan will be okay with it."

# CHAPTER 11
## OLIVER

Going to a stuffy charity gala feels like I just took ten steps back. But again, I'm here of my own free will, so maybe I should look at the situation as evolution not regression. At least, the venue is cool. It's my first time at The Los Angeles County Museum of Art, known as LACMA and at night, visitors get the full blast effect of the rows of California's lampposts in front of the museum's building.

There's a line of expensive cars in front of the place, waiting their turn to spit out the wealthiest people in town. I would be one of those clowns if Allan hadn't convinced me to take an Uber instead that dropped us off just before the line of cars started. I wish I could also avoid the red carpet and the step and repeat, but that will go against the brilliant marketing plan Garin has devised.

I didn't want Wreck of the Day to perform at a charity event. That's not the image we want to sell. They are a kickass rock band, not background music. I could have said no to Saylor. Actually, I'm looking forward for us to clash in the future. But I couldn't say no to Liv. So here we are. Garin's plan is to hold off any announcement Renegades Productions have signed the band. Instead, the story is that Allan and I attended this charity event, saw the girls playing, and we were hooked.

What I want to avoid is people linking Saylor to the mysterious girl caught in my arms in Hawaii. None of the paparazzi pictures were that clear. I want everyone to love Wreck of the Day for their awesome music, and not think they got a break because I was screwing the lead singer. It's fucking naïve, I know. We'll see how Garin's brilliant plan will work out.

I put on a show for the cameras as quickly as I can and enter the building. Saylor should already be there and I'm jonesing to catch a glimpse of her. I've avoided her since she came to my house to yell at me. I want her to think I'm only interested in a business relationship, something that couldn't be further from the truth.

Allan and I make our part and socialize for a while before we disappear to the green room where the band is lounging. My eyes immediately seek out Saylor and I find her in a corner talking animatedly with a tall bloke I've never seen before. Jealousy shows its ugly head and my impulse is to stride toward her and mark my territory. But that would be crazy, Saylor is not mine, not yet anyway. I have to keep it cool. So I take my time before I approach them.

When Saylor notices my presence, she tenses up visibly. However, I don't miss the elevator glance she gives me. I'm wearing a jacket and a tie. I bet she's remembering the last time she saw me in formal wear and how that evening ended for us.

"Good evening," I say.

The bloke talking to Saylor turns upon hearing my voice and gives me a genuine smile.

"Hi. So you're the infamous Oliver Best I've heard so much about."

"Oh?" I raise an eyebrow at Saylor.

She rolls her eyes and crosses her arms in front of her chest. "Not from me."

Ignoring her sharp response, I shake hands with the guy. My

jealousy dials down a notch when I don't sense any challenge in his demeanor. He's not after Saylor.

"The one and only. And you are?" I ask.

"Rodrigo Reinhardt."

"So, this event…"

"Organized by my family's company. Please don't say it aloud, though. I try my best to fly under the radar at such events. Pompous shenanigans are not my thing."

I like this guy already.

"So, you've met before?" I look from him to Saylor.

"Yes. I went to high school with Emma, Saylor's former roommate. The girls adopted me in a sense."

A striking brunette makes her way to Rodrigo and drapes her arm around his, totally staking her claim. She purposely ignores Saylor, as if she's not even there. She looks at me, and I know the instant that she recognizes me. I pray she won't be one of those birds who can't be around celebrities.

I notice the difference between Rodrigo and his date. Whereas Rodrigo seems to be a laidback bloke, this girl screams entitlement. She greets me with a simple hello, then she turns to Rodrigo.

"We should head back to the party, honey. Your mother would want you to socialize."

Rodrigo's shoulders slouch forward as if her request is a burden to him. "I suppose. It was nice to meet you, Oliver." He turns to Saylor. "Break a leg, Blue. I'm super stoked Wreck of the Day is playing tonight."

His date frowns and flattens her lips before she drags him back to the party. Once they are out of earshot, I glance at Saylor. "Wow. Talk about controlling females."

Saylor sighs. "I really don't like that girl. Rodrigo deserves better than that gold digger."

"You, maybe?"

My comment earns me a glare from her. "Not that it's any of your business, but Rodrigo is like a brother to me."

"Good to know," I say and regret immediately. Shit, there goes me keeping my cool.

"I should get ready for the show."

I'm not done with Saylor yet, so I scramble for something to say. "Are you playing any of your new songs?"

She looks at me, confused. "Uh, no. Allan said you didn't want us to."

Oh, shit. That's right. Fuck. I can't keep my head straight when she's around.

"I like the look you have going." I let my gaze drop down the length of her body, taking my time appreciating every single edge and curve of her.

Saylor glances down at her vintage 50s style dress which she paired with spiked heels. Total badass and the ensemble is giving me a boner already. I wish I could drag her to a private room and taste her cherry colored lips, feel her hand on my cock. *Fuck*. I need a cold shower now.

She shrugs. "Couldn't go all rock and roll on this crowd."

She begins to walk away but I place a hand on her naked forearm, stopping her. I see when goose bumps break out on her skin, and I hear her sharp intake of breath. Her beautiful eyes connect with mine and for a brief moment, there's heat and want in her gaze. I know I'm not imagining things. I take a step closer and lean forward so I can whisper in her ear. "You look amazing and you're going to kick ass out there."

I step away with difficulty. All my instincts are demanding I pull her closer to me for at least a kiss. It takes all of my self control to plaster a grin on my lips instead. Whatever is keeping her away from me, it's not lack of interest on her part. I didn't read her wrong in Hawaii, I didn't imagine the look of longing she gave me during Liv and Sebastian's wedding, nor the way she sang to me. She has fallen as hard as I have. But she's too stubborn and she won't tell me what's going on in her pretty head. I will find out one way or another, though. Without making a comment to my remark, she scurries away, joining Tabatha on the opposite side of the room.

I go back to the reception area, making a beeline to the nearest bar to order a drink. My heart is in over drive, my cock is still hard. I need to calm the fuck down. I order a double shot of whiskey and drink the whole thing in one gulp. Not enough. I order another one. The bartender is a pro and doesn't make any indication that my behavior is unacceptable. It's not until I have the second double shot that I start to feel more in control. That's when I notice a manicured hand on the counter. Curious, I turn to peer at my neighbor and I have to do a double take. The blonde woman next to me could have been Saylor's twin. She notices my stare and glances in my direction. Okay, she's not a total carbon copy, but similar enough to warrant my reaction. She has the same nose and high cheekbones, but her lips are not as full as Saylor's and her eyes are brown, instead of aquamarine blue. Her hair is also a darker shade of blonde.

"Hello, I don't think we've met," she says. "I'm Vanessa Holloway."

I blink a couple of times to get rid of my stupor. Even the voice is similar. Jesus fucking Christ. What was in that drink?

"Oliver Best," I finally say.

She narrows her eyes for a brief second and the small hairs on my neck rise. Her shrewd gaze is giving me the creeps. I can't believe I had her confused with Saylor even for a second.

"Oliver Best, the boy band singer," she continues.

"Yes, the one and only."

"I didn't peg you to be the kind of guy who enjoyed events like these."

"I was roped in."

"Oh, I hope not by a girlfriend." She smiles and peers at me through her fake eyelashes. Fuck, she's flirting with me.

"Nope. Business." I shift where I stand and look around, showing how not interested I am. I hope she gets the message.

"Me, too. Are you here alone? I wouldn't mind some company."

Jeez, straight for the kill. It's not something I'm not used to, but I would pass her proposition even if I was available. She has a weird vibe. I'm about to refuse her invitation when I feel a pair of eyes burning a hole through my skull. I turn and find Saylor a few steps back. She's rooted to the spot, frowning at me, right before her gaze shifts to the woman by my side—I already forgot her name. I don't know what Saylor sees, but her face goes as white as a sheet of paper. Without a word, she walks away.

"A friend of yours?" the woman asks.

I don't bother answering and go after Saylor, but I lose her in the crowd. Then a waiter jumps to a small podium in the center of the room and announces we can now enter the dining area. I search for Allan, but he must still be in the green room. I find Liv instead, looking all professional with a headset on her head and a tablet in her hand.

"Hey, Liv. How's it going?"

She looks up and and greets me with a smile. "Ollie, I'm so glad you could make it. Thanks for letting Wreck of the Day play here. You were a life saver."

"Not a problem. I haven't seen Bas. Is he coming?"

Liv scrunches up her nose. "No. He wanted to, but I asked him to stay home. He'd be a distraction."

I sense a note of tension in her answer and I file that away to ask Bas later. They just got back from their honeymoon. They can't possibly be having problems already.

"Alright then. I'll leave you to it. I'd better find my seat."

I'm relieved when I find Allan already at our table. I don't think I could handle making small talk with a bunch of strangers. The dinner goes by in a blur. I barely notice the food they serve, but I make sure my glass is never empty. I'm counting the minutes until Wreck of the Day's performance. That's why I'm here, after all.

# CHAPTER 12
## SAYLOR

No one notices that I'm having a mini freak out moment when I return to the green room. I stepped out for a minute in search of Liv, but instead I found Oliver talking to a ghost from my past. Even if I hadn't Googled my biological father when I found out about him, I would have recognized her. The resemblance is uncanny. No wonder Daddy dearest worked so hard to keep my face out of the papers. It wouldn't take much for people to make the connection. What is my freaking sister—I mean, half sister, doing here?

Vanessa Holloway is the epitome of the perfect daughter, at least that's what I could grasp once I came across her name in my search. She went to the best private schools, and graduated from an Ivy League university. She was everything I would never be, nor had the desire to be.

The question that keeps bouncing in my head is whether she knows about me or not? I doubt the Senator told her about his sordid past, but if I can see the resemblance between us, so can she. Did Oliver see that too? Was he attracted to her? *Ugh*. Stupid questions that shouldn't even be running in my head.

"Hey, are you okay?" Tabatha touches my arm to catch my attention.

"Yes, I'm fine."

Leaning closer so she can whisper in my ear, she continues, "Blue, you have to tell me when you are not feeling well, okay?"

I plaster a fake smile on my face. For once, it's not the damned clot in my head that's messing up my life.

"I promise I'm fine. It's just..."

Understanding dawns on her face. "Shit. It's him, isn't it? You fell for the guy."

I shake my head, but it's futile to deny it. Even a blind person could sense the crackling energy when Oliver is near me.

"I'll be fine. I just need to put on a good show. Music always fixes everything."

A strange glint shines in Tabatha's eyes. "Yes, music can perform miracles."

There's no time to analyze what Tabatha meant because Liv comes in next to explain the rundown of things. She's in the zone, extra professional, even if a tad stressed. I make a mental note to drag her with us after the gala for drinks. My friend needs some down time.

There's no introduction before we go up on the stage, we're nobodies after all, just the hired band. Since we can't play any of our original songs, our repertoire consists of classic pop and rock songs that appeal to everyone. I'm glad we don't end up playing to the walls and people actually take the dance floor. As gigs go, this isn't bad, but I hope it's the last. Wreck of the Day is meant for bigger things.

After the show, Oliver and Allan come talk to us, as we had arranged before. They're going to pretend this is the first time they've seen us play live. Such bullshit, but whatever. I know nothing about Marketing and PR. The whole time, Oliver can't take his eyes off of me. His gaze is making me all hot and bothered and I hate it. When I can't stand it any longer, I practically run back to the green room to collect my stuff. I need to get out of here, otherwise I'm going to combust on the spot. I don't see my half sister again, which is a blessing.

I hid my oversized bag behind some chairs because I don't trust security anywhere. I quickly look inside to make sure my wallet and cellphone are still there. That's when I find an envelope. Curious, I pull it out. My name is written in neat capital letters on the back, with no hint to who it's from. I rip the paper and I find a single note inside.

"I know your secret."

I snort and think which one? I've got so many it's getting harder and harder to keep up. This feels very much like a prank. I casually turn the note to look at the back before I toss it into the garbage bin, when I see the second part of the message scribbled there in a much messier handwriting.

"You and the ginger will pay for your deception."

My stomach bottoms out and I can't get any air into my lungs. I let the note slide through my fingers. This is not a prank. Someone out there knows that I lied to the police. They know that Mandy was somehow involved. What do they mean we will *pay* for it?

Panic seizes me and my vision becomes fuzzy. I was having such a good day, no migraine spells, no sickness. I take two wobbly steps toward the nearest chair and collapse on it, feeling my world go off kilter. If I close my eyes the dizziness will get worse. I drop my head between my shoulders and force air into my lungs. My heart is racing and there's a big lump stuck in my throat. *What am I going to do?*

I hear the door open, but I can't look up to see who just came in. Footsteps approach and a pair of expensive looking leather shoes appear in my line of vision. I don't need to bring my gaze up to know Oliver is standing in front of me.

"Saylor?"

My heartbeat increases, and there's elation there competing with the panic from before.

"What?" I try to put a bite in my response but it's a feeble attempt.

He crouches in front of me and my gaze automatically seeks

his. I don't find a devil-may-care attitude there, but worry mixed with pure longing. I take him by surprise—and myself—when I jump into his arms, holding on to him as if he is a lifeline. There's no hesitation on his part. His strong arms wrap around me, keeping me tight against his chest. I take a whiff of the smell that's solely his, the scent triggering the most wonderful memories, and I melt into him. I can feel the drum of his heart going at the same warped speed as mine. How did I ever think I could turn my back to this, to him?

♡ ♡ ♡

## OLIVER

I give Saylor a few minutes before I go after her. She bailed too fast after her concert and she didn't grant me the chance to congratulate her properly. Plus, I bet the green room will be empty right now. I should maintain my distance, keep the indifference field up, but I'm not one known for controlling my impulses.

I find her sitting on one of the folding chairs at the back of the room with her head lowered. Not a big deal but the fact she barely moves to the sound of the door opening makes me suspicious. Also, the noticeable rise and fall of her hunched back tells me she's taking deep breaths, as if she's having trouble breathing. *Fuck.* She has health issues, that I know, but she never trusted me enough to tell me exactly what they were. Not knowing drives me insane.

I close the door behind me and walk toward her. "Saylor?"

She doesn't look up and her lack of response doubles my worries. I crouch in front of her and finally, I see some movement on her part. She lifts her head and looks straight into my eyes. I'm gutted when I read fear in her beautiful gaze.

"What?" she asks, trying to sound annoyed, but failing miserably at it.

I'm taken over by a crazy impulse. I want to pull Saylor into my arms and protect her from whatever made her look so frightened. I'm a split second from doing so when she jumps into my arms, catching me by surprise. I fall onto my arse but my arms wrap around her lithe body, keeping her locked tight against my chest. My heart feels like it's going to explode the way it's beating at lightning speed. I'm not sure what's going on, but I'm not stupid enough to believe Saylor has had a change of heart. So I don't say anything and wait for her to make the first move.

We stay in that position for minutes, hours, not nearly long enough. She eventually pulls back, takes a quick look at my face, then slides off of my lap.

"I'm sorry about that." She stands up and fixes the full skirt of her dress, still not making eye contact.

I get up as well. "Do you want to tell me what just happened here?"

She brings a shaking hand to her forehead to rub it. "Not really."

I clench my jaw and count to ten silently, trying to keep a level head, but it's impossible. "So, what am I? A warm body for you to use and discard as you see fit?"

She whips her face in my direction, her eyes going wide. "Of course not."

"Really? I'm beginning to see a pattern here."

"We both agreed it was one week, Ollie."

The fact she just slipped and used my nickname works like a charm in melting some of my frustration and anger.

"Right. God forbid a change of plans."

She grabs her bag from the floor with a jerky movement and hoists the strap over her shoulder. "I'm not having this conversation with you."

She steps to the side to walk around me, but I hold her arm. "Fine. Let's not have this conversation. How about this? You work for me now, so I'm holding off any activity that involves physical exertion until I see your clean bill of health. That includes future shows and your music clip with Scott Rowan."

"What? You can't do that."

"Are you certain? It's my responsibility to make sure all talent can perform their tasks without putting themselves or others at risk."

She pulls her arm from my grasp and levels me with a glare. "You're such a jerk!"

"We established that the first time we met, didn't we, *darling*?"

Saylor opens her mouth, then clamps it shut again, clenching her jaw. Without another word, she stomps out of the green room and I don't feel an ounce of remorse for pulling such a douche move. I need to know if she's okay, otherwise I'll go out of my mind.

# CHAPTER 13
## SAYLOR

had plans to go out with the girls after the charity event, but with my frayed state of mind, I head straight home, calling Mandy on the way there. That note left me more worried about her than me. I can fend for myself, but who's going to protect her?

She's in high spirits on the phone, super excited about her classes this semester. The therapy is working. I decide not to set her back by talking about the note. I can't do that to her. It could very well be a prank.

By the next day, I've already convinced myself the note was most likely from one of Connor's former flings. I believe I did see one waitress last night who used to have a crush on him. There's absolutely no way someone knows the truth about the attack. The only person who could have babbled is long dead.

That leaves Oliver's crazy demand to occupy my mind and I find myself burning a hole through Tabatha's living room floor the next day as I pace back and forth.

"He has no right demanding that, no right," I say again for the umpteenth time.

"Actually, by the way he phrased it, he kind of does."

I turn to glare at her. "Whose side are you on anyway?"

"Yours, of course."

I resume pacing. "What am I going to do?"

"Uh, how about telling him the truth?"

I freeze mid-step. The thought has crossed my mind. But Oliver isn't stupid, he will know that's why I pushed him away and I'm afraid of what he'll do.

"No, that's out of the question."

"Then unless you know a doctor who would be willing to lie for you, I'm out of ideas."

"A doctor. Of course! I can't believe I haven't thought about it before."

"I was joking."

I can't tell Tabatha what I have in mind. I'm not even sure if he will agree to help me. I might have to tell him the truth. I grab my purse and make my way to the door.

"Wait, where are you going? I thought you came here to help me pack the garage." Tabatha frowns.

Guilt gnaws at my insides and I bite my lower lip. I already bailed last night and didn't help the girls with our equipment, a fact Tabatha mercifully hasn't brought up. Yet.

"I have to take care of this first. Oliver is hanging the music video with Scott Rowan over my head if I don't present him proof that I'm one hundred percent healthy."

"Blue, what are you planning?"

"I can't tell you yet."

"Fine. Don't tell me. But we're going to Renegades HQ later to make sure our stuff is where it should be."

"I'll be there. I promise."

Tabatha mutters something under her breath, but I'm already halfway out of the door and I can't hear what she said. I pull Derek's contact information and press the call button, hoping he will pick up my call. Things were super awkward the last time we saw each other.

"Hello?"

"Hi, Derek. It's me, Saylor."

"Yes, I know. Your name popped up on my screen. What can I do for you?" His voice has a tone of apprehension. Maybe he's worried I want to talk about Hawaii.

"I need to speak with you in person. Do you have some free time today?"

I have no idea what Derek's schedule is like. We totally lost touch after he and Liv split up. He's silent for a moment and my brain starts to spin some kind of bullshit excuse to convince him to see me. But he does reply after a while.

"Sure. I have a break in an hour. Could you meet me at the Children's Hospital?"

"Yes, I can do that."

"Okay, call me once you are there and I'll come meet you at the lobby."

♡ ♡ ♡

make it to the hospital in L.A. just in time and, as promised, Derek meets me in the main lobby, wearing a *Frozen* themed scrub. Even in the ridiculous ensemble, Derek turns heads as he walks in my direction. He was always a very attractive man and once upon a time, I truly wished Liv would fall in love with him. He would have been good to her, but the heart wants what the heart wants. Not that I don't love Bas, but at the time, he was the guy who had broken my best friend's heart.

Derek stops in front of me and nods all business like. "Saylor."

"Derek," I say in a mocking tone as I let my eyes roam through the length of his body. "Nice outfit."

My comment manages to remove some of the seriousness off his face and his lips twitch upward. "It's my favorite. The children also love it."

"I bet."

"So, you wanted to talk? Is everything okay?" Derek scans

my face and my guess is he's trying to decipher if I'm here to talk about Liv.

"Uh, could we go somewhere and sit down?"

"Sure, let's go to the cafeteria."

I let Derek lead the way, trying not to pay close attention to the people around me. I hate hospitals for a number of reasons, but a children's hospital is ten times worse. Most of the patrons in the cafeteria are parents who look bedraggled and depressed. I don't know how Derek can deal with this on a daily basis.

"Can I get you anything to drink? *Coffee*?" I don't miss the emphasis on the word and I smile. Derek still remembers my caffeine addiction.

"Sure, coffee would be great."

Five minutes later, he comes back with two cups and takes a seat across from me. I'm feeling nervous all of the sudden. What I'm about to ask Derek crosses all the lines. He takes a sip of his drink and waits for me to start, but when I fail to say anything, he breaks the silence.

"Saylor, you're beginning to scare me. What's going on?"

I take a deep breath and look into his eyes. "I need a big favor from you, Derek."

He frowns and rests his elbows on the table. "How come I have the feeling I'm not going to like it?"

"Because you know me too well?"

He shifts in his chair, leans back, and crosses his arms. "Go on."

"Wreck of the Day just signed with a music production company and we'll begin to record our first single soon."

"Wow, congratulations. That's great news."

"Yes, it is. But management is demanding a clean bill of health from me before they move forward."

"Okaay…"

"I need you to write me one."

Derek narrows his eyes and flattens his lips. "And you can't get that from your regular doctor? Why?"

I stare at the cup of coffee in front of me. "Because he won't be able to give me one."

"So, let me get this straight. You want me to write you a fake health certificate?"

"Yes."

I peer at Derek through my eyelashes, expecting him to bolt out of his chair at any minute, but he just sits there, watching me. After what it feels like an eternity, he finally speaks again.

"You know if I did that it could be the end of my medical career."

"I know and I wouldn't ask you if I had any other choice."

*You're such a fucking liar, Saylor. You have a choice.* I push my conscience's voice to the darkest corner in my mind.

Derek shakes his head and my heart sinks. "I can't help you, Saylor. I'm sorry."

I reach over and touch his arm. "Please, Derek."

"Saylor, why can't you get a legit health certificate?"

I pull my hand back and avoid his gaze. I knew I would have to confide in him if I had any hope he would help me.

"I have a blood clot in my brain and the doctor only gave me a year."

"Oh my God, Saylor." Now it's Derek's turn to reach out to hold my hand. "Is that the final diagnosis? Have you seen more than one specialist? I can refer you to the best neurosurgeons in the country."

I shake my head. "It's final. I'm resigned to it."

"No. I won't accept that. I want to see your CAT scan results."

"Derek, seriously, let it go."

He watches me through slits and I'm afraid he can sense I'm hiding something from him. "Do you want the certificate? Let me see your results, Blue."

My jaw drops. "Are you serious?"

He nods. "You know I am."

Shit. I should have known Derek wouldn't take my word for it.

"Okay. When should I bring them to you?"

"I'm slammed for the next couple of days. How about we meet on Thursday for lunch? You can pick the place."

"Sounds like a plan. I'll text you the address and the time."

I can't help it if my voice doesn't sound as enthusiastic as it should. I might have gotten Derek to agree to help me, but what will he do when he finds out I chose to die?

# CHAPTER 14
## SAYLOR

My phone begins to ring and my mother's name flashes on the screen. I'd better answer and get it over with.

"What's up, Mom?" I say as I walk to my car.

"Is that how you greet your mother?"

I roll my eyes and open my car door. "Hi, *Mom*. How are you, *Mom*?"

"Sarcasm duly noted. I've received an interesting call today from one of your father's minions."

"Ugh. I've already signed the papers. What more could they possibly want?"

My mother snorts. "For us to go live under a rock, far, far away from him."

"Fat chance of that happening."

"He's not pleased about your career choice."

"Of course he isn't. If he could ship me to Mars, he would. Well, he can suck it."

"I didn't tell them anything about your contract. But I thought you should be aware that your father might try to sabotage the band. He really doesn't want your face on the cover of every magazine and you know why."

Yes, I very well know why. I met the reason last night. But I don't tell my mother that. She would be furious if she knew.

"Thanks. I'll make sure to let my new bosses know about the Senator."

That's one secret I don't have to keep.

When I arrive at Oliver's place, I notice the absence of his car. I'm glad and disappointed that he isn't around. I ring the doorbell and Charlotte is the one who answers it. At least she's fully dressed today.

"Hi Saylor, your friends are already in the studio."

"Thanks." I walk past her and up the stairs.

When I reach the landing, I'm at loss for where to go. Where the heck is the studio? Why can't I remember?

"The studio is downstairs, in the basement," Charlotte says from behind me. "Do you mind if we have a little chat first? We didn't have the chance to talk properly the other day."

I look at her uncertainly. From what I understand, Oliver and Charlotte aren't close, so I don't know how much Oliver has confided in her. I hope she's not about to give me a lecture on how I broke her poor brother's heart.

"Sure," I say.

"You've pulled a number on my brother." Oh, hell, here we go.

"I'm not sure I follow." I watch her through slits and cross my arms.

"Oh, you do. Let's cut the crap. You and I both know the only reason Oliver signed your band is because he's madly in love with you."

"Excuse me?"

Charlotte waves her hand dismissively. "Oh, don't get your panties in a bunch. I'm not saying you don't have talent. My brother is not stupid. He wouldn't sink money on you if he didn't think you could make it big. I know I'm not close to him, but that doesn't mean I don't love him. Ollie is, well, he's been messed up for a very long time. If you care for him, you'll be real with him."

My initial animosity toward Charlotte diminishes considerably. "The last thing I want is to hurt him."

"Because you love him." Not a question, but a statement. I could lie. I *should* lie. But I can't.

"Yes."

Charlotte's expression remains impartial, as if my confession means nothing to her. "Okay, that's all I needed to know." She walks away, leaving me confused as hell. What was the point of this conversation? Make me feel guiltier than I already do?

I shake my head before I go downstairs. As I get closer, I can hear the muffled sounds of instruments. Inside, most of our stuff is already unpacked. I remember this room vaguely, it used to be an entertainment area with a couple of big couches and a pool table. I fucked Oliver here a few times, but I'm glad it has been completely remodeled. I don't need to be haunted by memories. It's bad enough I have to be in his house every day now.

The girls all look at me when I enter the space, but it's Tabatha who speaks first.

"It's about time. Where have you been?"

"Running errands."

My vague answer makes Tabatha give me the stink eye. I ignore her.

"Check out these keyboards, Blue. They are top of the line," Remi says excitedly, running her fingers over the brand new instrument.

"It looks awesome."

I glance around, searching for our old instruments, but there's no sign of them. "Where is Rita?" I whip my face in Tabatha's direction.

"Relax. It's over there." She points at a couple of stacked up boxes in a corner. Next to it, I spot my guitar case and I release the breath I was holding.

I stride toward it, picking it up almost reverently. My guitar is everything to me. It has helped me through more hard times than I can count. The thought reminds me of the conversation I had with Mom and I cringe internally. I have to warn my friends.

"Guys, I have something to tell you." I return to the middle of the studio, still holding my guitar.

"Oh, shit. It's bad news, isn't it?" Remi takes a seat on a comfy looking leather chair.

"You don't know that." Sticks comes closer.

Remi looks pointedly at her. "Nothing good ever begins with 'I have to tell you something'."

"What is it, Blue?" Tabatha asks.

"Well, it's about my biological father."

"Oh great, what did that asshole do this time?" Tabatha says.

"Uh, I'm lost here, guys. Who's your father?" Remi looks at me.

I take a deep breath before I reveal to Remi and Sticks I'm the illegitimate daughter of a Senator. Tabatha has known about the man for a while now. I skip over the part about the attack because, honestly, who would want to talk about that? All I say is I've renounced any rights I might have had over his name and fortune.

"Man, what a story," Remi says after I'm done with the details.

"I take it you didn't share all of this with us for nothing," Sticks points out.

"No. One of his minions contacted my mother. Apparently, the Senator is not happy about my chosen career. He must have heard we played at Reinhardt's charity event." Most likely, my dear sister told him. "I don't think he knows yet that we have a contract with Renegades, but I wouldn't put past him to create problems for the band."

"You need to tell Allan and Oliver then," Remi says.

"I plan to, but I just wanted to give you a heads up first."

Tabatha narrows her eyes in defiance before strumming her bass. "The Senator can bring it. Wreck of the Day is not going anywhere."

# CHAPTER 15

## OLIVER

wanted to be around when the girls came by to check out the studio. The company I hired to transport their instruments brought them to the HQ Saturday night after their unofficial debut concert. But Allan wanted to meet with me. He had something urgent to discuss and he didn't want to do it at Renegades.

I meet him at Closing Time, the pub in Hermosa Beach where Wreck of the Day used to play. Right now, in the middle of the day, it's pretty much dead. I find Allan sitting at a booth in the back, his shoulders hunched forward as he cradles his beer glass.

I slide into the seat opposite him and pull my sunglasses up. Allan looks at me with a frown. "It took you long enough."

"Sorry, mate. I got here as fast as I could. What's going on?"

Allan slides a folded note across the table in my direction. I pick it up and read the one-liner out loud. "I know your secret." I raise an eyebrow at him.

"Read the back."

"You and the ginger will pay for your deception. What's this?"

"You tell me. I found it on the floor of the green room last night. Any secret you've been keeping that you want to tell me about?"

I shake my head. "Wait? You think this note was for me?"

"Uh, yes. The ginger reference is what clued me in." He points at his own hair.

I read the note again while my brain grapples for an answer. It takes me a minute to realize this note wasn't meant for me. "Shit."

"What?" Allan sits up straighter.

"Bloody hell, it all makes sense now."

"What does? Jesus, Ollie. Don't leave me hanging like that."

"This note wasn't meant for me. I think someone is threatening Saylor."

"Saylor? But why?"

Saylor's awful past comes to my mind. Her name was never released to the papers. What if someone wanted the truth to come out? I don't know for what purpose though. Why would someone hold a grudge against her? And the ginger? Are they referring to her former neighbor, the one she was seeing last year?

"I don't know, mate. But we have to find out. Do you know a good PI?"

"A PI? What the hell for? Shouldn't we talk to Saylor first? If her life is in danger, we should go to the police."

"I'll talk to Saylor, but I don't think she wants the police involved."

Allan leans back on his seat and clenches his jaw. "I'll make some calls. I have more bad news."

What could be worse than someone threatening Saylor's life? My impulse is to get the hell out of this pub and go check on her.

"What now?"

"It's about Scott Rowan. I sent him the new songs we have for Wreck of the Day and he hates them all. He wants to use one of his own."

I narrow my eyes at Allan. "You told me the deal with Scott was for him to record an original song by Wreck of the Day."

"It *is* the deal. Scott is being a diva right now. Anyway, I'll work with him, but it wouldn't hurt to have new material to show the guy. In reality, we need a ballad and none of the songs I sent him were."

"You want Saylor to sing a ballad with Scott Rowan?" My voice comes out as a growl.

Allan raises both hands. "Whoa. Take it easy, tiger. It's just a song. I'm not suggesting they do the horizontal tango on screen."

*Close enough*, I want to say, but I'm already acting like a lunatic, I don't need to add more crazy to it. "Mate, you need to stop with the mid-century references. Do the horizontal tango? Who the fuck talks like that?"

"That's not a mid-century reference," Allan says through clenched teeth.

"Whatever. I gotta go."

I walk out the pub without looking back. *Shit*. Now I have two very unpleasant topics to discuss with Saylor. I wonder which one she will take more offense to, the fact I know about the threatening note or that Scott Rowan hates her music?

When I arrive at Renegades, I've decided to talk about business first, but when I open the door to the studio, I only find Tabatha and Sticks there.

"Where's Saylor?" I ask.

Tabatha turns to me with an eyebrow raised. "Saylor and Remi had a shift at the Goulas and left half an hour ago."

"It's Monday. I thought the restaurant didn't open on Mondays. Besides, why are they still working there?"

My question doesn't please Tabatha and now she's openly glaring at me. "Because they have commitments. They can't simply bail on their employer without notice."

"Without notice…" I pinch the bridge of my nose. "It's been weeks since you signed with my company."

"So? We haven't even recorded anything yet and you haven't announced that you signed Wreck of the Day."

It's clear I won't win any arguments with Tabatha, so I decide to drop the subject for now.

# CHAPTER 16

## SAYLOR

didn't think it strange when a few weeks back Dimitri said the Goulas was going to open today, a Monday, and asked Remi and I to work a shift. He'd said it was a private party event. Ten minutes into our shift we discover the private event is in fact, a party for us. Dimitri hands us shots of ouzo and removes our aprons himself. The restaurant is filled with Remi's family—including her Japanese grandparents—and their close friends. That means the place is packed.

In the blink of an eye, tables and chairs are shifted to create a long-ass table in the middle of the restaurant and Remi and I are given the seats of honor.

"What is going on?" I say in a daze as Remi's grandma pushes me toward my chair.

"What do you think, child? It's not every day not one but two of our family members get the opportunity of a life time."

I'm taken aback by her statement. "I'm family?"

She stares at me like I've lost my mind. "What kind of question is that? Of course you are family."

I take my seat next to Remi and a glass of red wine materializes in front of me. I lean closer to her and whisper in her ear, "Did you know about this?"

"Nope. They sure kept it under wraps and coming from my family, that's a huge accomplishment."

"You don't say."

The Goulas has always been a loud restaurant, but tonight it's a cacophony of sounds with everyone speaking at a higher voice level. I'm asked so many questions it's a miracle I manage to get any food and drink inside my body. Well, drinking the wine is easier, and a couple of hours later, I have a great buzz going on.

I shouldn't even be surprised when Oliver walks into the restaurant. It's like destiny is trying its hardest to shove us together. He has a look of pure surprise on his face as he takes in the room, which clues me in he had no idea a party had been planned.

His gaze connects with mine and I can't look away. My entire body hums, my heart rings at his mere presence alone. My fuzzy brain can't remember why I keep pushing him away. He begins to walk in my direction, and with unsteady legs, I get up to meet him half way. I'm lucky I manage not to fall flat on my face. We stop within inches of each other and I smile like a fool.

"Hi."

"Hello, sugar. Didn't know you were having a party."

"It's a surprise farewell party. Isn't it great?"

Oliver narrows his eyes, but on his lips there's a ghost of a smile. "Yes. How much did you drink?"

I wrinkle my nose. "I have no idea. A lot?"

"Oy, Oliver is here!" Someone shouts and I turn to glare at the stupid person who interrupted my conversation with him. I want to keep Oliver all to myself. I've missed him so much.

"Hey, Pepe. How are you?" he says.

"Wonderful. Took the missus on a very nice vacation thanks to you." He winks at Oliver and then turns to smile at his wife.

Before anyone decides to say hello to Oliver as well, I take his hand and drag him outside.

"Whoa. You kicking me out?"

"No. I was hot. Didn't you think it was hot in there?" I pull the front of my shirt forward to let some cool air in. I don't miss when Oliver's gaze drops to my chest.

He chuckles before he answers. "A little bit. I don't think I've ever seen this side of you before, Saylor."

I frown at him. "What side?"

"The funny drunk side."

I pout and cross my arms in front of my chest. "I'm not a funny drunk."

"Okay, sugar. Whatever you say. Come on, let's head back inside before they think I've kidnapped you."

He moves closer and touches my lower back, pushing me forward, but I'm not ready to go, not by a long shot.

"Wait. You didn't tell me yet why you are here."

"What makes you think I wasn't invited?"

"You weren't."

"Touché." He takes a step back and runs a hand through his hair. "I came to talk to you, but we can wait until tomorrow."

I step closer, invading his personal space, and touch his chest. I stare at it for a moment, enjoying the feel of his accelerated heart beat under the palm of my hand, before I peer at him through my eyelashes. He swallows hard and on a crazy impulse, I lick the hollow of his throat.

"Saylor, what are you doing?" His voice comes out as growl.

"Making sure you still taste as good as I remember."

His hands grab my arms and I'm afraid he's going to push me away, but he doesn't.

"You're drunk. You'll regret this tomorrow."

I rise onto my tiptoes and kiss his jaw. "Tell me you don't want me to kiss you and I'll step away."

I keep on placing feathery kisses on his jaw, on the corner of his mouth, while Oliver stays rooted to the spot, unmoving. But his self-control doesn't last long. His hand finds its way into my hair. He grabs a handful and tugs it, pulling my mouth away from his skin. He stares at me intensely before he crashes his lips against mine for a wild, merciless kiss. After all this time without him, his tongue tastes like the purest nectar, it infuses my body with heat, and I want to meld myself to him. With his free hand, Oliver pulls me flush against his body and I can't miss the bulge of his erection pressing against my belly. I want to touch him, but he has me locked tight against his body. I can't move, I can't do anything besides be lost in his kiss.

A car honks in the background and Oliver pulls away. His breathing is shallow and his gaze is feverish, wild. Even in the darkness I can read the desire in his eyes.

"Oliver..."

He takes another step back, increasing the gap between us.

"We can't do this, Saylor. Go back inside. We'll talk tomorrow."

"I don't want to."

"Sugar, you'll thank me later."

He turns on his heel and before I can stop him, he's already sliding inside his car. He peels out of the parking lot as if the devil is after him.

*Shit. What have I done?*

# CHAPTER 17

## OLIVER

drive for hours, only going back home around four in the morning. Once there, I take a cold shower and still I can't fall asleep. She kissed me. She fucking kissed me and I couldn't do anything besides run the hell away. What other choice did I have? I couldn't take advantage of her while she was drunk. But damn if it didn't kill me to leave her behind while all I wanted was to get her into my car and fuck her until she screamed my name from the top of her lungs.

I head to the studio down in the basement. The place is immaculate, as if no one was ever here. All boxes have been emptied, flattened out, and disposed of. I turn the light on but keep it dimmed, and venture into the room. Saylor's beloved guitar is in its case, propped up against the wall next to the amps. I touch the weathered case, but I know better than to open it. I got everyone brand new, top of the line instruments, everyone except Saylor. She would never have traded Rita—her guitar—for anything else.

I keep walking until I reach the acoustic guitar mounted on the far wall. This one I bought on a whim. I dabbled with the instrument when I was in high school, but I never got to play well enough to attempt a performance in public. No, the guitar had been Sebastian's thing.

Still, I take the instrument from its place and sit on the leather couch, propping it on my knees. The first strums reverberate so loud in this empty room that they almost startle me. It takes me a few attempts before I can actually make a tolerable sound with it. Before I know it, I'm playing the only song I ever learned, *Faith* by George Michael. In high school, Bas was the casanova, the brooding guy every girl was in love with. So I bet with him that if I played this song, I could score more girls than him. I can't remember if I did or not. I screwed my way through the female population of that prep school like I was on a mission, broke more fucking hearts than I could count. I was so rotten.

I don't know how long I mess with the guitar, but I wake up with someone shaking my arm. I open my eyes with a start and sit up, not knowing where I am for a second.

"Relax, dude. It's me. Did you sleep here?"

Charlotte peers at me with a smirk on her face and a cup of coffee in her hand.

I rub my eyes. "What time is it?"

"Ten o'clock."

"Bloody hell. Why did you wake me up then?"

"Because Allan is already here, working like a bee."

I grab her coffee and take a big sip of it.

"Hey! That wasn't for you."

I stand up and keep the beverage out of her reach. "Too bad. Shouldn't have awakened me."

"You're such a jerk."

I give her a toothy grin and walk out the door. Since I'm awake, might as well see what Allan is up to. I head to the common area—I can no longer call it the living room—and I find the guy already glued to his laptop. He has his headphones on, completely oblivious to the world around him, as he listens to his favorite tunes.

I clap his shoulder and he almost falls off his chair. Pushing his headphone off, he looks at me, startled. "Jesus fucking Christ, Oliver. You almost gave me a heart attack."

I pull up a chair and peer at his laptop screen. "What are you doing working so early?"

"It's ten in the morning. Garin asked me for content for the press release about Wreck of the Day. He thinks he can pitch a story to *Teen Vogue* provided that we can release a single within a couple of weeks."

"Also, the CW is looking for songs for one of their new shows. They love up-and-coming bands. If they pick Wreck of the Day, that might even mean an appearance in one of the episodes."

"It sounds like we need a couple of hits, then," I say.

"I really like the song they ended their show with at Ray's Venue. The audience responded really well to it."

"Good. We can book studio recording time as soon as Saylor provides her clean bill of health."

"Uh, what? You didn't tell me you were asking the band that."

"No, not everyone, just her."

Allan stares at me through slits. "Why?"

"Because she's fainted a couple of times in my presence."

"Oh, shit. You don't think she's pregnant, do you?"

"No." Not that it would be the end of the world if she were.

"Okay then. I'll remind Saylor today."

"Good, you do that. I'm going to grab some breakfast. Do you need anything?"

Allan shakes the white plastic bottle next to him. "No, thanks. I'm good. I've got my protein shake."

I roll my eyes. "Suit yourself. I'll see you in a few."

# CHAPTER 18
## SAYLOR

wake up with the mother of all hangovers. My mouth is dry and it tastes like there's something rotten inside. Slowly, I open my eyes and find out I fell asleep on my bed with last night's clothes on.

*Ugh. Last night.* I have a vague memory of attacking Oliver's mouth outside of the Goulas. Did that really happen? I can't remember the last time I drank to the point of amnesia. I want to believe that it was all a dream, but the tingling sensation on my lips tells me that we did kiss.

*What am I going to do?*

A knock on my door interrupts my mini freak out moment.

"Saylor, are you up?"

The voice is muffled and my slower than usual brain takes some time to recognize it. "Yes, who is it?"

"It's me, Mandy."

"Mandy?"

I'm out of my bed in a flash, almost tripping over my discarded shoes as I stride out of my bedroom. I cross the small living space and take notice of its state of disarray. No time to worry about it now. I open the door all the way with a jerky movement, startling poor Mandy who had been looking away from it.

"What are you doing here? Did something happen?"

Mandy looks at me like I've lost my mind. "Jeez, how much did you drink last night? Did you forget about our breakfast date?"

I search my brain and come up empty. "Was it today?"

Mandy shakes her head and pushes me out of the way as she ventures into my small house. "Boy, I can't believe I missed last night's shenanigans."

She stops in the middle of my living room and places her hands on her hips. "What happened here? Were you hit by a mini tornado?"

My gaze skids around the messy room. It definitely wasn't like this before I left the house yesterday.

"Something like that. If only I could remember. My brain is fuzzy as hell."

Mandy turns to look at me. "Come on. Hop into the shower and put some clean clothes on. I'm hungry."

"Where are we going?"

"Some place down in Hermosa Beach one of my classmates told me about. I've been dying to go for ages."

"Ugh, okay fine. Feel free to spread some of your organizational magic powers around." I give her an impish grin and she rolls her eyes.

"You know I will. I can't stand messy places. I swear if you hadn't forgotten about our date, I would say you left your room untidy because you knew I was coming by."

"Are you implying I'm taking advantage of your compulsive cleaning behavior, *Monica Geller*?"

Mandy throws a pillow at me. "I'm not Monica! Now shoo before I leave without you. Did you miss the part where I said I was *hungry*?"

♡ ♡ ♡

An hour later, Mandy parks on a side street near the shore, and we walk to the café in Hermosa Beach she can't stop gushing about. My headache has intensified, and now I have hunger pains to add to this fantastic morning. There was no coffee left in the kitchen at the Goulas residence by the time we left and my caffeine deprived body is running on fumes.

I'm never drinking again.

It's already past ten in the morning and for a Tuesday, it's pretty crowed. All tables outside are taken.

"They're too busy. It will take forever for us to get any food. Let's go to McDeath."

"No way. I didn't drive all the way here for nothing." Mandy keeps on walking and I have no choice but to follow her.

I'm distracted and don't see when she stops abruptly, so I bump into her.

"Wha—"

"Hey, isn't that Oliver?" She points at a table at the far end of the outside area.

I follow her gaze and sure enough, Oliver is there, sitting alone at a table with his sunglasses on and a cup of coffee in front of him. He seems distracted, looking out at the ocean. A big knot forms in my throat and my heart does several back flips. Of all the cafes in Hermosa Beach, Mandy had to bring me to the one Oliver prefers. That's just great.

Before I realize what Mandy is doing, she's already walking in his direction.

"Where do you think you are going?" I whisper as I trail after her.

"I don't think we'll get a table any time soon and I'm starving."

"I don't want to sit with him."

My reply falls on deaf ears, and it's too late to bail without Oliver seeing us. He has already turned his face in our direction.

"Hi, Oliver. Do you remember me?" Mandy greets him and I frown at her back. When did she become this outgoing person?

"Mandy. Of course I remember you. How's it going?"

"Pretty well. Are you here alone?"

Oliver tilts his head lightly and I know that he's looking at me now, even with the sunglasses. "Yes. I'm here alone. Would you like to join me? I just put my order in."

Mandy is already pulling up a chair. "If you don't mind. Saylor is in a piss poor mood, and I'm afraid that if I don't give her coffee soon, she will bite my head off."

"You don't say. Too much red wine last night perhaps?"

There's no teasing smile on his lips and I swallow a snarky remark. He's angry at me and he has every right to be. I can't believe I threw myself at him last night.

"Yes, it seems so. The Goulas are party animals. I can't remember a thing." I lie. Some details are fuzzy, but I vividly remember kissing him last night.

Oliver only nods, he doesn't make a comment to my statement. I wonder if he believes me or not.

The waitress returns to our table and I order a large cup of coffee before anything else. Five minutes later, after small talk carried on by Mandy and Oliver, my friend excuses herself to go the restroom, living me alone with him.

I pretend to be very busy with my coffee.

"I came to the Goulas last night. Do you remember that at least?" Oliver asks casually.

"Yes." I don't make eye contact.

"Bloody hell, sugar. You can look me in the eye."

I glare at him. "It would be easier if you didn't have your sunglasses on."

He pushes the accessory up his head. "Better now? Listen, you don't need to walk on eggshells around me. What happened last night wasn't a big deal. We have a past, you were drunk, it was just a kiss. No harm, no foul."

My jaw drops. Here I was worrying he would be pining over me. It seems he has truly moved on, despite what his sister says.

"I'm sorry about that. It won't happen again."

He takes another sip of his coffee before he continues, "I actually came to the Goulas last night because I wanted to talk to you."

I lean back and cross my arms. "If you're going to ask about my health certificate, I already got an appointment with my doctor."

"No, it's not about that, but it's good to know. We need to start recording A.S.A.P. There are two things I want to discuss with you. The first is about the collaboration with Scott Rowan. He didn't like any of the songs we sent him. I believe they are too edgy and different from his style and we want to meet him in the middle."

"What exactly do you have in mind?"

"A ballad."

If Oliver had asked me to write a slow song a few months ago, I would have had no problem doing so. But writing a love song in my current state of mind, I don't know how I'll be able to do it without revealing it's about him.

"When do you need it?"

"As soon as possible."

I groan and look at the ocean. I'm a professional. I can do it.

"What's the second thing you wanted to discuss with me?"

Oliver glances over my shoulder. "We can talk later."

I follow his gaze and see Mandy coming our way. He already mentioned my faux pas so whatever he wants to discuss with me won't have to do with our relationship. We just talked business which leaves me dying out of curiosity. What does he want to say that he can't in front of Mandy? I guess I'll just have to wait.

"I want to tell you something as well," I say.

Oliver raises an eyebrow at me. "Okay. Go ahead."

"Nah, we can talk later."

I smirk at him. I could tell him about the Senator in front of

Mandy. She knows about him, too. But I couldn't pass up the opportunity to tease Oliver as well.

"Touché."

He finally grants me a smile and my stupid heart reacts accordingly. *Moronic, useless muscle.*

# CHAPTER 19

## OLIVER

I decide to order my breakfast to go and leave the beach side café as fast as I can. I came there for some time alone with my thoughts, and being around Saylor so soon after that damn kiss is not helping me get my mind in order.

I was glad she didn't react badly to my news that Scott Rowan didn't like any of her songs. Maybe she was still feeling too mortified about the kiss to give me any grief over it. I almost told her about the note I found then and there, but in hindsight, her friend's interruption worked out for the best. That wasn't the right place to drop the bomb on her.

In the end, I didn't need solitude but a busy day at work. Who knew I would enjoy working behind the scenes of the music industry so much? The day goes by fast and I don't even notice how late it is when Charlotte comes bouncing into the living room, all dolled up to go out.

"What are you guys doing? It's past eleven o'clock."

I give her an elevator glance and raise an eyebrow at her. "And where are you going this late on a Tuesday night?"

Charlotte rolls her eyes. "Seriously? I'm meeting friends for drinks, not that it's any of your business."

"Whatever. I thought you wanted to move to L.A. for school, not for a change of party scenery."

"Who says I can't do both? Besides, I can only start school next semester. I need to occupy my time."

She heads to the door and Allan shuts off his laptop.

"I should get home. I'm beat."

I'm ready to hit the sack myself. I know the girls were using the studio today. I heard them practice earlier, but Renegades HQ is ultra quiet now.

I turn off my laptop as well, but before I head to my room, I take the stairs down to the basement. I don't know why I feel the need to check the studio out, everyone must be long gone. There's a faint light coming from under the studio's door. Someone must have forgotten to shut it off. I push the door open, expecting to find the room empty, but I see Saylor sitting on the couch with an acoustic guitar propped on her knee and a piece of paper next to her. She looks up when she hears me.

"What are you still doing here?" I ask.

"How late is it?"

"It's almost midnight. Allan just left."

She puts the guitar away and stretches her arms. "Shit. I lost track of time."

My eyes involuntarily drop to her chest and I try my best to keep my cock from reacting as I walk closer.

"Are you working on the ballad?"

Saylor drops her arms to the sides and lets out a sigh. "Yes. It's awful."

"Impossible." I pick up the sheet she had been working on.

"No, it really is. I haven't written a ballad in a long time."

I pull up a chair and take a seat in front of her. "Play it for me?"

Saylor's eyes widen a fraction as panic seems to flitter in her gaze. *What is she afraid of?*

"Come on. It can't be that bad."

"Alright. But you can't rescind your contract after you listen to this."

"I won't." I smile, hoping to encourage her.

She picks up the guitar again and plays the first two verses of her work in progress. I didn't know how much listening to her sing, accompanied only by an acoustic guitar, would affect me. My heart is thundering in my chest and I'm afraid she can hear it from where she sits.

"I told you it was bad."

I shake my head to get my brain to work again. "No, it's not bad at all. I like the melody, but maybe we could tweak some verses in the lyrics."

"We?" She raises an eyebrow.

"What? You don't think I can help?"

"I didn't know you dabbled with music composition."

I shrug. "I picked up a thing or two during my stint in Boys Future."

She stares at me as if trying to decipher whether I have ulterior motives or not. "Okay. I'm stuck anyway. Maybe your raw talent can help."

Several possible replies pop in my head but I refrain from speaking any of them out loud. They are all filled with innuendo and I don't want to go there.

We work together for another hour and I manage to put my feelings for Saylor on the backburner. Who knew writing songs could be so interesting? When I catch her trying to suppress a yawn, I decide to call it night.

"It's late and I think we made good progress. We can continue tomorrow."

"Yes. I'm beat."

"If you're too tired to drive, you can crash here. You know I have a spare bedroom." Saylor looks at me through slits and I can guess what's she's thinking so I continue, "Or I can get you an Uber."

"I can drive. I'm not that tired." Another yawn sneaks in.

"Right. You worked all day and you're still recovering from a wild night. You're not driving. Period."

"You're not the boss of me." She crosses her arms in front of her chest and glares at me.

I smile, ready to contradict her, but she realizes her mistake and adds on, "I'm mean, you are, but not in that sense."

My smile grows bigger.

"Ugh. Stop smiling. You know what I mean."

I stand up and stretch my arms and back. "I'm not sure what you think is going to happen if you spend the night. I have every intention to sleep like the dead tonight. I'll keep my bedroom door locked in case you can't be trusted to control your urges."

I shouldn't have teased about last night, but her expression of indignation is priceless.

"Are you going to hold that lapse of judgment over my head forever?"

"Nah."

Her face turns serious and that wipes the smirk right off of my face. "I need to tell you something. It's personal."

My first thought is she's going to tell me about the threatening note she received. So I sit back down and mirror her somber expression. "Go on."

"You know that my biological father is a politician, right?"

"Yes. Bas has filled me in."

"Well, when I turned twenty-one, he made me sign an official document giving up all my rights to his fortune in exchange for keeping my name out of the newspapers when the attack happened." Saylor glances down and licks her lips. "It was all self serving, anyway. He doesn't want the press to ever know about my existence. It would put a blemish on his impeccable rep sheet."

"He's a bastard and doesn't deserve to have you as his daughter."

She peers at me through her thick eyelashes and my chest

tightens. I want to pull Saylor to me and hold her close to my chest. She needs to know I will always keep her safe.

"Thanks. Well, as you can imagine, he's less than happy I decided to play in a band. You see, he has a daughter only a few years older than me and, well, we look very much alike. You actually met her at the charity gala."

I'll be damned. That woman at the bar. I thought I was losing my mind then. Now everything makes sense. My mind begins to spin and I have a nagging suspicion where that note came from now. I will wait until Saylor finishes what she has to say before I bring the subject up.

"And because the resemblance is so obvious, he will try his best to keep me in obscurity."

"Do you think he will create problems for the band?"

"Yes."

"Does this have anything to do with the threatening note you received?"

I see the moment the words leave my mouth that Saylor wasn't planning on saying anything about that.

"How did you know about the note?"

"Allan found it on the floor of the green room. He thought the note was meant for me. But it was for you, wasn't it, sugar? Do you think your sister put it there?"

Saylor stands up suddenly, her body now as tense as a coiled spring. "The note has nothing to do with my half sister."

I stand up as well so I can better glower at her. "What is it about then?"

She pushes past me and grabs her purse from the floor. "It's none of your business."

Whoa, what's with the one-eighty change? I go after Saylor, grabbing her forearm and spinning her around. I won't let her escape so easily this time.

"Don't you dare give me that bullshit. Someone is threatening you and that makes it my damn business."

"Because I'm your *investment*." I don't miss the venom in her tone.

"No, you stubborn woman. Because I love you and I would die before I let anything happen to you."

Saylor's eyes widen at my unintentional confession. Since I already screwed up with the charade, I might as well go for the kill. I cradle her face between my hands and kiss her like this is the last time I will ever be able to. She doesn't resist, her lips and tongue surrender to my invasion as her hands wrap behind my neck. My entire body responds to her and before I know it, we tumble onto the leather couch, me on top of her, between her legs. This feels like déjà vu, Saylor giving into her deepest desires when she's feeling cornered. She will try to run away tomorrow, I can count on it, but right now, I just want to feel her on my tongue, plunge my cock into her heat.

I grind my pelvis against hers, while my fingers trace the side of her torso until they reach the underwire of her bra. I leave her mouth long enough to open the front of her button down shirt and admire the swells encased by her lacy underwear. With the tip of my fingers, I circle her nipple, making her throw her head back and moan with her eyes closed.

"Oliver..."

"Yes, sugar."

"I want your mouth on me."

"Where?" My voice comes out as a groan.

"Everywhere."

Fuck me. Like she even needs to ask. I bring my face between her breasts and swipe my tongue across one mound. "Wish granted."

I open the front clasp of her bra before capturing one of her nipples with my mouth. I suck and tease, making small circles with my tongue while Saylor moans softly. My rock hard erection is straining against my jeans and I think I'm going to explode if my cock is not buried deep in her sheath in the next second.

"Sugar, I need you naked right now otherwise I'll lose my mind."

To my surprise, Saylor pushes me off of her and I end up falling flat on my arse. *Shit. Did I go too far?*

♡ ♡ ♡

## SAYLOR

I shouldn't be doing this, but my body and my heart have wrestled away the feeble control my mind had. It's pointless to fight. I want Oliver with every fiber of my being, I love him more than he will ever know. It was easy to shove the want and the feelings to a dark corner while he kept his distance. Little did I know that Oliver had the power to break all my barriers and bullshit with only three simple words. *I love you.*

Now, I'm a goner. No turning back. I want him to claim me, to do as he pleases.

"Sugar, I need you naked right now otherwise I'll lose my mind." His warm breath spreads over my nipple, making the throbbing between my legs almost unbearable.

I push him off of me so I can get rid of my clothes, but I'm too eager and he ends up on the floor. Now he's looking at me like somebody just stole the candy out of his mouth.

"Oops, sorry. I didn't mean to do that."

The relief on his face is priceless. "Thank fuck."

He crawls back to me, opening my legs to nestle between them. His face is inches away from my crotch.

"I can feel your heat even through all your clothes. But they need to go."

He pushes the zipper down, parting the fabric with his hands. I lift my butt so he can easily peel my jeans off. Once only my panties and bra are left, Oliver runs his hands up my legs, leaving a trail of goose bumps behind. His fingers play with the seam of my panties and I begin to feel impatient.

"Oliver, if you don't fuck me with your fingers and mouth, I'll have to take care of it myself."

"Bossy."

He pushes my panties aside and run his tongue over my swollen bud. I arch my back. "Fuck. I need more."

He's only too eager to comply by inserting two fingers at once and sucking my clit until I can't see straight. I'm stretched so thin, so deprived of his touch that it doesn't take long for me to come. The orgasm hits in the next second is intense and swift, it liquefies my bones. It makes me scream his name over and over again.

"That's it, sugar. Come all over my tongue," he says.

He keeps sucking my clit and pumping his fingers in and out even after the last tremors of my release have gone. If he continues, I'm going to come all over again.

"I need you inside me, Ollie."

He's on his feet and out of his jeans in record time. It's almost comical. Then he searches for something inside of his jeans pockets and a moment later, looks at me. "I don't have a condom here."

I stand up and grab his shaft, pumping it up and down before letting it go and sauntering away toward the door. "You better go get it then."

"Where are you going?"

"Your room, of course. I want to be fucked properly and that ain't happening on that small couch."

In reality, I don't think I can work in this room with the girls tomorrow knowing I slept with Oliver in here. I don't even make two steps into the hallway before he throws me over his shoulder and makes a run for his bedroom.

"Ollie, what are you doing? Put me down." I laugh.

He throws me in the middle his California King-size bed and I bounce on the soft mattress. Next, he points his index finger at me. "Bra and panties off."

Not waiting for me to comply with his demand, he disappears inside the bathroom, coming back a few seconds later with a box of condoms in his hand.

"What's all that?"

"We've lost a month. Need to catch up."

"You want to catch up on sex?" I lean on my elbows, trying to suppress the laughter wanting to breakthrough.

"Damn straight." He frowns. "Why are you still wearing your bloody underwear?"

I pull the straps of my bra down and throw it to the side. Oliver is already in bed, condom wrapped around his swollen cock, ready to go. He nudges me back gently only to fall between my legs next.

"I'm still wearing panties," I say as he nuzzles my neck.

"Are you?"

There's a yank followed by the sound of fabric tearing and I can feel the head of his erection at my entrance. "Oliver, did you just rip my panties off?"

He looks into my eyes with a devilish grin on his lips right before he plunges inside of me in one precise push, scrambling all my thoughts.

"You bet I did. You can't say I didn't warn you."

He stops any protest I might have with his mouth. I bring my knees up and cross my legs at the ankles, caging him in, allowing him to go deeper like that. The satisfied grunt that comes from deep in his throat makes me even hotter for him. His cock is rubbing me just in the right spot and I'm hit by another devastating orgasm within minutes.

"Oh my God. Don't stop. Don't ever stop fucking me, Ollie."

"I wish I could comply, sugar. But you feel too good."

He keeps pumping, faster and harder until his cock grows bigger inside of me and I feel the tremors of his release. He bites my shoulder as he plunges even deeper and I come yet again, screaming so loud this time I bet his neighbors can hear me.

"Fuck," he says before he collapses on top of me, hiding his face on the crook of my neck, and breathing hard.

He stays in that position for a couple of minutes, unmoving but the rise and fall of his chest. When his breathing is back to normal, he rolls over and pulls me close.

"That was…fuck.'"

"I know," I say before I start to pull away. I need to use the bathroom.

"Running away already? You didn't even wait for me to fall asleep this time." I hear the hurt behind the attempt at a joke.

"Ollie…"

I sit up on the bed and he does the same.

"I'm done playing games, Saylor. You know where I stand. I love you and I'm not going to hide my feelings anymore to make things easier for you. If you don't reciprocate them that's fine. Just say it to my face so we can both move on."

My chest is tight. My heart is on the verge of short-circuiting for not knowing how to react. It's rejoicing and breaking at the same time.

"Is that what you think? That I don't care for you?"

He shrugs as if it's of no consequence if I love him or not. But his eyes, they tell me a different story.

I move closer to him and touch his cheek. "The truth is I wish I didn't care for you. I wish that my heart wouldn't sing every time you are near me. I love you so much it hurts my soul."

He closes his eyes and lets out a shaky breath before he kisses my open palm. When he looks at me again, there are so many emotions in his gaze that I can't begin to take them apart.

"I'm fucked up, but you know that already. I won't promise you every day it will be perfect with me, but I'll try my damn best to do right by you."

I kiss him so he won't see the tears already forming in my eyes, or the guilt. It's a soft kiss at first, but it quickly becomes clear it will lead to another round of mind shattering sex. So I pull away and jump out of bed.

"What—"

"I wasn't trying to run away before. I have to use the bathroom."

Oliver falls against his pillow and picks up the box of condoms, shaking it for my benefit. "Good. Hurry back, we still have these to go through."

"Optimistic, aren't you?"

"No. Realistic. I'm a stud. I can go on all night long. I hope you can keep up."

I laugh and shake my head. "Alright, *stud*. Challenge accepted. The one who falls asleep first cooks breakfast tomorrow."

"You're on." He smiles and my heart crumbles.

I just bought my ticket to Hell. I might have lost the battle against my feelings, but I'm still not telling Oliver that he's in love with a dead woman walking. I want him to be happy for as long as I have. The burden of the truth I must carry alone.

# CHAPTER 20
## OLIVER

"I have nothing to wear," Saylor looks at what's left of her panties.

"I don't mind if you go commando," I say from my vantage position on the bed.

Saylor glares at me in all her naked glory, giving me another boner. I just fucked her in the shower and before that when we woke up. I shouldn't have any juice left despite my claims from last night.

"I'm not going commando wearing skin tight jeans. I will get a rash."

"Fine. You can borrow a dress from Charlotte."

Any other bird would probably balk at the idea, but not my Saylor. Without a word she leaves my bedroom and a moment later, returns wearing a long, bohemian dress with a plunging neckline and bare back. Charlotte texted sometime in the middle of the night to let me know she went to San Fran with her friends and she won't be back until Sunday. It suits me fine. I want as much time alone with Saylor as I can get. I give her an appreciative glance and smile.

"Fuck, you are beautiful."

Her gaze zeroes in on my erection and she raises an eyebrow.

"Don't get any ideas. I'm not riding you again until you make me breakfast."

"Excuse me? I think you are the one who needs to get your ass into the kitchen A.S.A.P. You fell asleep before I did."

She puts her hands on her hips and levels me with a glower. "You dropped dead still inside me last night. I had to roll you over and get rid of the condom."

That could have happened. Saylor wore me out.

"Ugh, fine." I throw my legs to the side of the bed and get up.

I open the top drawer of my chest and pull out a pair of briefs. I'm taken by surprise when Saylor yanks the underwear from my hand. "Nu-uh. If I have to go commando today, so do you."

"Oh yeah?"

"Yes."

I tackle her and we both collapse on the bed with me on top. She lets out a yelp before she starts to hit my chest. "Ollie, cut it out. I'm hungry."

"Me too, for your sweet pussy." I kiss her neck as my hands lift the dress up.

"You just had my pussy." She tries to wiggle out from under me.

I tickle her and I know it's game over when she stops putting up resistance. But voices coming from the living room interrupt our morning fun.

"Shit," we both say in unison.

I roll off of Saylor and she gets up, fixing the dress. It's wrinkled beyond hope now.

"It sounds like Allan and Tabatha. What are we going to tell them?"

I lean on my elbow and grin from ear to ear. "You look so cute when you're flustered like that. The truth of course."

"Which is?"

I sit up and pull her to me, my arms going around her tiny waist. "That you belong to me and I belong to you."

"God, were you this corny before we hooked up?"

"No. See what you did to me? You've ruined my game beyond repair, now you must keep me forever."

She wrinkles her nose. "I didn't realize you had a 'you break, you buy' policy."

"Oh, yes, I do, sugar. I'm afraid you're stuck with me now."

## SAYLOR

I feel Tabatha's judgmental glare the moment I step foot in the living room with Oliver in tow. I must have painted on my face what I have been up to.

"You're here early. Working hard on your new song?" Allan asks, still oblivious I spent the night.

Oliver throws an arm around my shoulder and kisses me on the cheek before turning to Allan. "Something like that."

The ginger's face turns beet red when he finally catches on. He clears his throat and turns to stare at his laptop.

"Good. I would like to book recording studio time as soon as possible. I'm trying to get your debut single in one of the CW's new shows."

"Wow, really? That'd be amazing."

"I was just telling Tabatha that I hired a new stylist."

My friend turns to Allan and glares at him. "And I already told you I'm not happy about that. We don't need a makeover."

"I'd be down for a makeover," Remi says as she joins us in the open room.

"Where did you come from? I didn't hear the doorbell," I say.

"Uh, Oliver gave us keys yesterday. He didn't give you one?"

I whip my face toward him. He is already in the kitchen cooking breakfast. "No, he didn't."

"Oops, must have slipped my mind." He smiles like an imp and my eyes narrow to slits.

"Right."

"Hey, is that a new dress? It's gorgeous." Remi's comment makes my face flush. Shit, I so do not want to explain why I'm wearing Charlotte's dress to her.

"It sure is."

We all turn to stare at Oliver's sister, who just stepped onto the landing. What's up with everyone making surprise appearances?

"Char, didn't you say you were going to San Fran and wouldn't be back until Sunday, or did I imagine that?"

"I changed my mind last minute." She struts across the room to sit on the high stool by the kitchen island and begins to eat the pieces of fried bacon Oliver has already put aside.

"I told Saylor she could borrow some of your clothes. I hope you don't mind." He bats her hand away from the food.

Charlotte's shrewd gaze hits me square in the face before she turns to Oliver. "Why, may I ask, did she need to borrow clothes?"

Oliver comes back into the living room, holding a plate of scrambled eggs and bacon. He hands me the plate with a smirk, and I hope he can see the murderous glance I'm giving him in return.

"Because I may have gotten a little too impatient last night."

"Wait? What? Did you…"

"Yes, Oliver and I are back together. Can we talk about something else now?" I say while my face is in flames.

Remi reaches us in two long strides and hugs Oliver and I both. "Yay! Finally. I knew you would work things out."

She steps back and eyes my plate. "Oh, that looks yummy. I hope you made enough for everyone, *boss*."

"Sure, help yourself."

We hear hurried footsteps coming up the stairs, and a moment later, Sticks appears on the landing, looking flustered and out of breath.

"Sorry, I'm late. I overslept and hit major traffic coming here. What did I miss?"

Sticks for once is not wearing her baseball cap and her long hair is still damp and hanging loose. I'm about to ask her 'late for what' when Allan stands up and looks at her as if he's seeing a ghost.

"I know you," he says.

Sticks turns to him, her face now ashen.

"Your mother used to work for mine," he continues. "You tried to teach me how to play the drums. Now I feel like an ass for not recognizing you. Why didn't you say anything?"

She shrugs and looks away. "I didn't think it mattered."

"Hey, stop making her feel bad for your memory issues," Remi says.

Allan's face turns a deep shade of red and he rubs the back of his neck. "Sorry. I didn't mean it like that. Did you all know?"

Tabatha and I nod, and Remi says, "Yup."

Allan turns to Oliver but he just raises his hands up and takes a step back. "I know nothing, mate."

"Jeez, you guys are so full of drama. I'm beat. I'm heading to bed. Saylor, you can keep the dress. It looks better on you, anyway," Charlotte says as she makes her way to the guest bedroom.

"Uh, did I miss anything? What is Sticks late for?" I look at everyone.

"As I was saying before, I hired a new stylist and the only free time he had for a consultation was this morning. I sent you a text last night. It was last minute, my apologies."

As if on cue, the doorbell rings.

"That must be him," Allan says.

I follow Tabatha's lead and take a seat on one of the office chairs. A minute later, a petite Asian man with a mop of bright blue hair walks into the living room. He removes his sunglasses with a grand gesture and takes his time looking at each one of us.

"Good morning, everyone," he finally says.

"Tabatha, Saylor, Remi, Sticks, this is Monni, one of the best stylists in the world." Allan introduces the man.

My jaw drops of its own accord. He can't be serious.

"Aw, Allan. You're always so kind." Monni pats Allan's shoulder affectionately before turning to us.

"Nice to meet you, ladies. Are you ready to have some fun?"

Remi and I trade glances and she mouths O.M.G. to me. My eyes catch Oliver's expression across the room. He's fighting to keep his grin suppressed. I turn my face to the man in front of us again. He paired tight jeans with a button down shirt and a hot pink scarf wrapped around his neck. The long sleeves of his shirt end in big ruffles, reminding me of flamenco dresses. Every single finger on his hands is adorned by a ring, some heavy on the bling. Does the guy think he looks stylish dressed like that? I'm not sure about fun, but today promises to be a very interesting day.

# CHAPTER 21
## SAYLOR

onni, the world famous stylist, with his blue hair and bright veneer teeth, turned out to be a freaking genius. That should teach me not to judge anyone's talents by their appearance. After the initial shock of meeting him for the first time, he proved to us he knew what he was talking about. He used to work for a major design house in Milan as their brand director before he decided to go solo. Within five minutes, he had won all of us over, including Tabatha.

Yesterday, we spent the day in a fancy hair salon in Beverly Hills, getting plucked and buffed until we looked like a million bucks. None of our makeovers were anything drastic, Monni just gave us a better version of ourselves. My long hair stayed long, the hair stylist only trimmed the dead ends and I got a Brazilian keratin treatment to add some shine to it.

Tabatha got bronze highlights that turned her jet black hair dark brown. The lighter color did wonders to soften her face.

Sticks surprised me when she asked to dye the tips of her hair purple. Monni proved he's in this business for a reason. He suggested an ombre effect, and instead of purple, Sticks's natural brown hair faded into a rich burgundy color. The result was phenomenal.

The only time there was a bit of tension was when Monni bickered with Remi after she insisted on keeping her skater girl look. He said her fashion choices were clashing with the overall image of the band, which is rock and roll chic, but she would not budge. In the end, they compromised, and Remi let Monni add a few essential elements—according to him—to her style.

Today, we have a photoshoot scheduled with an upcoming photographer because the band needs official photos to use in promotion. Riley Michaels is her name, a petite blonde with bob-length hair and lots of energy. I liked her immediately.

My hair and make-up are all done, but I'm still wearing a white robe. Monni comes in with a portable rack and there are several expensive looking outfits hanging from it. Attached to each hanger, I see a tag with my name.

Monni turns to Richard, the make-up artist. "Oh, I love what you've done to her face. Stunning."

"Well, it's easy when the canvas is already flawless." The guy winks at me and I blush.

"I second that," Oliver says and my mouth hangs open. I was hoping he wouldn't be here. I'm still getting used to the idea that we are together and Oliver doesn't know how to keep his hands to himself in public.

"Boyfriend?" Richard asks.

I don't know what to say, but Oliver answers for me with a resounding 'yes'.

"Lucky girl." Richard gives Oliver an elevator glance while he has his back to us, perusing the outfits hanging from the rack.

He pulls one out, inspects it for a moment, then turns to Monni. "This is the one."

"I had a feeling you would choose that one," Monni says.

I crane my neck to see the dress Oliver has selected. It's a leather mini that looks too small to fit me. Oliver catches me staring and smiles.

"Would you mind trying it on, sugar?"

I get up and take the hanger from his hand. "Sure."

The studio is an open warehouse, so there aren't any rooms with closed doors. The 'changing room' is nothing more than a corner protected by a partition. At least there are mirrors in here. I drop the robe to the floor and wiggle my way into the dress. It's as tight as I predicted but at least it doesn't have a plunging neckline. I actually look badass in it.

Oliver sneaks in and looks at my reflection in the mirror before stopping behind me. "This dress was made for you." He runs both hands over the sides of my body and my skin breaks out in goose bumps. I close my eyes and imagine them going up my dress and touching me in other places.

He kisses my exposed neck at the same time his fingers dig into my waist, pulling me flush against his bulging erection.

"Ollie, we can't…"

"I know." He bites my earlobe, eliciting a moan from me.

A throat clearing behind us has me jumping forward and out of his reach. Riley is standing there just outside the partition.

"Sorry to interrupt, but we should start soon."

There's a small grin on her face when I walk out, and that makes me even more mortified.

"Sure. I'm ready."

Oliver pinches my butt when he walks by and I reward him with a glare. All he does is wiggle his eyebrows up and down in response.

I've never been to a photoshoot before, but I quickly discover it's not as glamorous as people make you believe. It's hard work and tiring. The bright lights are hot and we constantly need our make-up refreshed. I'm sweating like a pig underneath the dress and not even the industrial fan Riley has pointed at us is helping cool off my skin.

"Alright, guys. We're almost done with this round," she says.

"Wait? *This* round?" Remi says under her breath.

Riley gives as a few more directions and then calls for a

break. I step out of the spotlight with glee. The leather dress is glued to my body and I can't wait to get out of it.

Monni tells us we have three more looks to go through before we are done and we all grumble in unison. I search for Oliver in the vast warehouse. I thought his presence would make me uncomfortable, but after a while, I forgot he was there. I find him in a corner, having a conversation with Allan. I wonder when he got here. Next to me, Sticks makes an undecipherable sound and walks in their opposite direction. I'm almost one hundred percent sure there's more to the story between her and Allan than she's letting on, but it's not my place to ask.

I veer first toward the refreshments table to grab a bottle of water and a bite to eat, but my attention is still on the power duo. Allan tells Oliver something he's clearly not happy about. I can tell by the way Oliver runs his hand through his hair in a jerky motion.

"What's going on?" Tabatha appears next to me, her gaze trained on them as well.

"No clue."

In silent agreement, we stride in their direction. Their conversation halts abruptly when they notice our approach and it raises all sorts of red flags in my head.

"Hey, Allan. I didn't know you would be here too," I say.

"Yes. I had some news that I wanted to deliver in person."

"You don't sound too happy," Tabatha says.

"It's about Scott Rowan."

"Let me guess. He didn't like the new song either." I glance at Oliver who has a rare somber expression on his face.

"No, on the contrary. He loved it. But he won't be able to record the single with you any time soon."

"Why the hell not?" Tabatha asks, ready for a fight. I wouldn't put it past her to jump on a plane and drag Scott Rowan here, by his hair, if necessary.

"He got into a car crash earlier this morning. Broke a few ribs and one of his legs."

"No way!" Remi says as she joins our group. "Poor, Scott."

"What are we going to do?" I ask.

"Well, there's nothing we can do now," Tabatha grumbles.

"Actually, I just suggested Oliver step in and sing the duet with you."

"What?" I say at the same time that Remi says, "That's a great idea."

Tabatha narrows her eyes at Oliver. "Hum, I don't know."

"Guys, it will be perfect. The media will love it, especially when they find out Saylor and Oliver are together." Remi clasps her hands together, excited like a little girl.

I hope she sees the stink eye I'm giving her. I so don't want my love life dissected by the press.

"I told Allan it would be up to the band. It won't hurt my feelings if you say no." Oliver looks pointedly at me.

"I thought you were retired," I say. It's lame, but it's the only response I can come up with right now. I don't know how I feel about recording the single with him yet. We have already mingled our professional and love lives enough.

He shrugs. "One never completely retires from this business."

I turn to Tabatha and Remi, searching their faces for a clue to their thoughts. Remi is totally onboard. It's pretty much down to Tabatha and me because I don't think Sticks would care one way or another. Tabatha must have sensed my dilemma and stares straight into my eyes.

"I'm okay with it if you are, Blue."

Great. Now I'll be the bad guy if I say no. I turn to Oliver again and my chest tightens a bit. His facial expression seems indifferent but his eyes tell me a different story. There's something vulnerable and expectant in their depths. He might claim he won't care if I say no, but I don't think that's true. That helps me make my decision.

"Let's do it."

# CHAPTER 22

## SAYLOR

After cancelling on me two times, Derek finally has time to meet me at a café near the Children's Hospital. He's fifteen minutes late, but mercifully, he's wearing regular clothes, not his Disney character scrubs.

"Sorry to keep you waiting. It's almost impossible to escape the hospital. It usually takes me an hour to make it from my department to the front door."

Derek has always been super dedicated to his goals, but right now, his hard work is actually showing. He has dark circles under his eyes and has also lost some weight. He still looks like a Calvin Klein model though.

"You work too hard."

"When you are holding people's lives in your hands, there's no other option but to work hard. Now, enough about me. Let me see your CAT scan results."

Jeez, so much for small talk. I hand him the large envelope and Derek quickly pulls all the beautiful pictures of my brain. His lips flatten and his eyebrows furrow as he examines the images. Then he looks at the written report. I can tell when he realizes my case is not inoperable, as I had led him to believe.

He glances up and I don't know what to make of his expression.

"You are choosing to die." His voice has a hint of disbelief.

"It's not that simple."

"It is that simple. Why?"

"Because the possible outcomes of brain surgery terrify me, okay? I don't want to become a vegetable."

"Jesus, that's the worst case scenario possible."

"But it can happen."

He pinches the bridge of his nose and looks down at my results again. "Your clot is not in an area difficult to reach. A good surgeon would be able to extract it with minimum damage to brain tissue."

"But there would be some damage."

"So, you would rather die? Think of all the things you will miss out on."

I look away because I don't want Derek to see my tear filled eyes. "You don't think I know that?"

Derek reaches out and grabs my hand. "Saylor, let me refer you to another specialist. My mentor Dr. Laurent is a brilliant doctor, considered one of the best brain surgeons in the country."

"Derek, please. Don't insist. I've made up my mind. Are you going to help me, or not?"

He pulls back and flattens his lips. His blue eyes are dark and calculating, and I'm afraid he will go back on his promise. Oliver hasn't broached the health certificate again, but I know he will if I don't present him one.

After what it feels like an eternity, Derek pulls an envelope from his messenger bag and slides it across the table. "Here's your certificate."

I retrieve the envelope quickly before Derek changes his mind and shove it in my bag.

"Thank you, Derek."

He shakes his head. "I can't believe you're doing this. You

need to tell Liv at least. She deserves to know she won't have her best friend around for much longer."

His words make the guilt in my heart grow exponentially, becoming almost unbearable. If I tell Liv she will never accept my decision.

"You still love her, don't you?"

Derek's frown turns deeper. "This has nothing to do with my feelings for her. And no, I'm no longer in love with Liv, so wipe that pitying look off your face."

"So, are you seeing someone?"

Derek flattens his lips and crosses his arms. "Are you seriously asking me about my love life right now?"

"What? It's better than listening to you lay the guilt trip on me."

He rubs the scruff on his jaw before he flags a waiter.

"No, Blue. I'm not seeing anyone. I don't have time to date."

"Make time, Derek. You'll never know what life can throw at you."

"Only you could say that with a straight face." His lips twitch up, but the levity on his face disappears in the next second. "You'll be missed, Blue."

♡ ♡ ♡

Derek and I have a drink before we part ways. He urges me again to go see his mentor and I flat out refuse. By the way he squares his shoulders and grinds his jaw, I have the feeling he won't give up so easily. The worst he can do is to breathe word to Liv, but I know he won't. Not only because by doing so he'd expose what he did and ruin his medical career, but because Derek has honor. Something I'm obviously lacking.

I head straight to Renegade's HQ. The girls are already there, jamming away, and Oliver and Allan are working like busy bees on their laptops and phones. I wait until Oliver ends his call to hand him the envelope Derek gave me.

"My clean bill of health as per your demand." My tone has more bite to it than I intended and Oliver frowns. He takes the envelope from my hand and throws it on the pile of paper already on his desk.

"What? Aren't you going to read it?"

"Of course not. It says you're one hundred percent healthy, it's good enough for me. Come here." He pulls me closer, caging me in between his strong arms and legs.

My heart tightens, and not because of our proximity, but because of the guilt that's eating it away. The drive did nothing to help me shake off the feeling and Oliver's reaction just made it much worse. A knot forms in my throat and my eyes burn. I'm going to lose it in front of Oliver so I lean down and kiss him. I wonder if he can taste the sadness on my lips.

With each stroke of his tongue against mine he manages to lighten the weight crushing my chest. I ignore that Allan is nearby and sit astride on Oliver's lap, bringing my body even closer to his. He senses the shift in me and stands up, with me still latched onto his frame.

"Where are two going?" I hear Allan ask, but I refuse to open my eyes and acknowledge him.

Oliver breaks our kiss long enough to tell him we'll be right back. He takes me to his bedroom and locks the door.

"Ollie, I need you so much." I say between kisses. I don't mean his body in this moment, I mean him as a whole.

"Take whatever you want, sugar." He places me on his bed before he grabs his T-shirt by the back and pulls it off. His jeans go next.

I skim out of my own, pulling my panties down with them at the same time. Oliver stares at my half naked body with such hunger in his gaze that he makes me speechless. Without bothering to remove my top, I open my legs for him and he groans right before he collapses on top of me. The tip of his erection teases my entrance right before rubbing against my clit.

"Stop torturing me. Put the condom on already."

Oliver nuzzles my neck just before he bites my earlobe. "Are you still on the pill, sugar?"

"Yes," I whisper.

"I haven't been with anyone else since Hawaii."

"Me neither." I feel I have to say it as well.

Oliver leans back to stare into my eyes. "I love you so bloody much, Saylor."

I raise my head to kiss him because I can't deal with his love declarations right now. It's making everything so much worse. With my hand, I guide his cock back to my entrance and Oliver takes it as sign that the condom will be damned. I always find myself breaking all my rules with this man, but today, I don't care. My pussy is so wet, he enters me with ease, making my entire body tingle. I bite his lower lip as he begins to move in and out, terribly slowly.

His hand trails down my belly until his fingers find my clit. He begins to make slow circle motions, making it really hard for me to keep quiet. I don't want to come so fast, I want to make this moment last longer. I pull his teasing hand away and manage to roll us over, so now I'm on top.

Oliver smiles at me as his hands dig into my hips. "I love when you take charge."

I gyrate my hips slowly even though the throbbing between my legs is urging me to move faster. Now it's my turn to tease him. I clench my internal walls, milking Oliver's cock. He closes his eyes and lets out a guttural groan.

"Are you okay there, babe?" I say, breathless.

"Fuck, you're gonna kill me." He tries to set a faster pace by moving my hips with his hands, but I put a stop to it.

"Nu-uh. No cheating."

"Fine." He brings his upper body up and captures one of my nipples with his mouth.

I don't know what's worse for my self control, his fingers on my clit, or his tongue and teeth teasing my hard nub. I begin to move faster without even realizing it. When the orgasm hits, I bite his shoulder so my screams are muffled.

"God, you feel so good," he says before his body tenses and I feel his release filling me. With a final grunt and push, Oliver falls backwards, pulling me with him.

We stay glued like that until our breathing returns to normal. We are wet and sticky, but I wish we could stay like this forever. Eventually, I roll off of him and lie on my side. Oliver imitates my position and rests his chin on his closed fist, staring at me with a cat-that-ate-the-canary grin. With his free hand, he plays with one of my nipples.

"I know that I'm irresistible, but you can't jump me every time you see me, you know. I'm your boss after all."

I let my fingers run along his torso with a light feather touch. "And what will my punishment be, boss?"

He grabs my hand and brings it to his lips for a kiss. "I have to think about it. Right now, it's shower and get back to work before Allan has a nervous breakdown."

♡ ♡ ♡

When we return to the common area half an hour later, Tabatha is there talking to Allan. She glances in my direction and stands up. Her eyebrows are furrowed and her lips are nothing but a thin flat line.

"Saylor, can I have a word with you for a moment?"

I sense a lecture in my near future, but I guess I deserve one. I follow her back down to the studio and find it completely empty.

"Where are the girls?"

"They went out to grab something to eat." Tabatha closes the door while I make a beeline for Rita.

Without making eye contact, I ask, "What's up, Tabby?"

"Allan told me you gave Oliver your clean bill of health." It's impossible to miss the contempt in her tone. "I understand you don't want people to know, but you're with Oliver now. That's not right."

I put Rita aside and glare at my friend. "I can't tell him the truth. You know why."

She throws her hands up in the air. "Yes, I know why. But it doesn't make it okay. You were already crossing a line before. Now you are just being a selfish bitch."

I wince at Tabatha's outburst but she doesn't stop there.

"What do you think is going to happen when your condition gets worse, when you can no longer hide you are dying?"

"I don't know! I haven't thought that far yet."

"I'll tell you what's going to happen. Oliver is going to lose his mind. That man is head over heels in love with you, and I know you feel the same way about him."

I hide my face between hands and feel the tears that are threatening to burst loose. "I don't want him to suffer before-hand. I want to make him happy, even if it's only for a short while."

Tabatha sits next to me and forces me to look at her. "Go see another doctor, Blue. Please."

I stand up abruptly and put some distance between us. "What's up with everyone today trying to make me change my mind? Derek said the same thing."

"Derek? Shit, Saylor. Is he the one who gave you the false certificate?"

"Yes."

She stands up as well and crosses her arms in front of her chest. "You are taking this too far. It's going to blow up in your face and it won't be pretty."

"You know what? I can't be here." I stride toward the door.

"What are you doing? Running away again?"

I ignore her jab and walk out the door.

# CHAPTER 23
## OLIVER

don't know what Tabatha had to talk with Saylor about, but it must have been bad, because she left soon after and didn't return. I called and texted her and all I got was one lame text back saying she needed some time alone. I tried to get Tabatha to explain what the hell had happened, but she was also not cooperative. That was yesterday.

I went to bed alone for the first time since I got Saylor back, and I didn't like it one bit. As a consequence, I'm in a sour mood this morning. When I make my way to the open area, Allan is already there.

"Good morning, boss."

I grunt in response.

"Can we talk before everyone gets here?"

"Sure, mate." I veer into the kitchen to make some coffee. I barely slept last night.

"The PI I hired to look into that mysterious note came back with his first report."

That peaks my interest. "Any leads?"

"I haven't looked at it yet. I was waiting for you."

I haul my ass back to where Allan is, forgetting my caffeine fix for the moment. Allan opens a manila envelope and pulls from it not a stack of papers, but a stack of black and white photos.

"What the bloody hell are those?"

"Uh, I have no idea."

I start to go through the photos, while slowly, my blood begins to boil. It looks like the PI had actually being stalking Saylor.

"I didn't ask him to follow her."

"Me neither. I guess he was being thorough."

My hands freeze when I see a picture of Saylor having a beer with the bloke who almost ruined my mate's wedding, Liv's ex-boyfriend. I run through them all like a maniac and by the time I come to the last picture from the stack, my pulse is jamming in my ears and I have bile in my mouth.

"What the fuck was she doing with him?" I ask out loud.

"Who is that?"

I jump out of my chair and make a grab for my key fob.

"Where are you going?" Allan sounds alarmed.

"To get fucking answers."

♡ ♡ ♡

try my best not to stomp the gas pedal, but my blood is pumping and giving myself limits is something completely foreign to me. It's not even ten in the morning yet so I'm hoping to catch Saylor at home. I arrive at the Goulas' residence at the same time Saylor is coming out the front gate. She freezes upon seeing me. I purposely park my car at an angle in front of hers, blocking it in case she wants to bail before explaining herself.

I'm out in the next second, my body as tense as a coiled spring. I'm not making any attempt to hide how fucking angry I am. She notices my murderous expression—how could she not—and she takes a step back. *Shit*. I don't want her to be afraid of me.

"Ollie, did something happen?"

"What were you doing with Liv's ex-boyfriend the other day?" I stay close to my car and the gap between us feels like a chasm.

Her face blanches at the same time her eyes widen. "What?"

"You heard me. What were you doing with that guy?"

She narrows her eyes at me and crosses her arms in front of her chest. "How do you know I met with Derek?"

Ah, that is his fucking name.

"I doesn't matter how I know. You looked pretty chummy with him."

Saylor breaches the distance between us, her gaze now sparking with fury. "I'm going to ask you again, Oliver. How did you know I met with Derek? Did you have me followed?"

Fuck. I guess I didn't think things through.

"It's not what you think."

She takes a step back and throws her hands up in the air. "Oh, my God. You *did*. How dare you?"

"I was worried about the note you received so I asked Allan to hire a PI to look into it. The guy followed you of his own accord. I didn't order him to do it."

"You hired a PI?" Saylor pulls her hair back and begins to pace. "I can't believe you did that. It's just unbelievable."

"I was fucking worried about you!" I take a step in her direction but she raises a hand, signaling me to stop.

"It doesn't make what you did right. I can't even look at you right now."

I don't mistake the disappointed tone of her voice, and it guts me like nothing else. I knew I would screw things up, I just didn't know how fast.

"Please remove your car. I need to get out of here."

"Where are you going?"

She levels me with a glare. "I'm going to work. We have a record to finish."

## SAYLOR

Son of a bitch. I can't believe Oliver hired PI and had me followed. For a moment I thought he had found out about the blood clot and my decision, but it turned out he was just suffering from major misplaced jealousy. I shouldn't be pissed, I'm the biggest liar in this whole mess, but I can't help the feeling. He invaded my privacy, whether with good intentions or not.

I don't know how I managed to drive back to Renegades HQ in one piece. The altercation has left my entire body shaking and my head is now throbbing. Nausea hits out of nowhere and I almost don't make it to the bathroom. Luckily, there's one next to the studio in the basement and nobody is around yet. When I go up the stairs, Allan stares at me with a guilt stricken expression.

"Is everything okay?"

"I can't talk to you right now. I have work to do." I make a beeline for the fridge to get some chilled water so I can take my medicine for the migraine.

"Where's Oliver?"

"Don't know. Don't care."

With bottled water in hand, I head back to the basement, and try my best to control my ire. I don't want to talk about the pictures or the argument with Oliver. As always, l let the music work its miracle, I let it cure my sorrows. When the girls arrive, I don't engage much with them. Tabatha is still upset with me and acting aloof. Fortunately, Remi and Sticks are oblivious to the tension.

We practice the new songs, and after our lunch break, I decide to head to the beach for inspiration. I need to compose at least two more songs and I can't find my muse locked in that basement. I leave Rita behind, because what good would a guitar be without amps, and grab the acoustic guitar mounted on the wall instead. The sun is out, but we're finally experiencing a little bit of autumn chill. I'm wearing a short dress for once and the soft breeze leaves goose bumps on my skin in its wake. I pull the zipper of my hoodie all the way up, which is enough to ward most of the cold away. I didn't have the foresight to bring a towel, and when I sit down, the cold sand is a little bit of a shock against my skin. I keep the guitar on my lap, conscious not to get any sand on it, and stare out at the ocean. But instead of finding peace, my chest feels heavier, and my eyes prickle. *Damn it*, I didn't come here to cry. A single rogue tear manages to escape the corner of my eye and I quickly wipe it off. A moment later, Allan finds me.

"Saylor, may I sit down?"

"The beach is public."

He crosses his legs and sits next to me. "Don't be mad at Oliver. This whole PI mess is my fault."

"Wasn't it Oliver who asked you to hire one?"

"Yes, but not to investigate you."

I take a deep breath. "This is all for nothing. The note was most likely a prank."

"You didn't receive any new ones?"

I shake my head. "Nope."

"I hope you are right, Saylor. But if you do receive another threat, will you please let me know?"

I turn to look at him. "Why, so you can run and tell Oliver?" I can't keep the bite out of my tone, even though I know Allan has good intentions.

"No. Because I don't want anything to happen to you. If you have a stalker we need to deal with it. They are dangerous."

"It sounds like you have experience."

"Not me, but my mother. It can get nasty."

Allan is right, I shouldn't shove this matter under the rug if it happens again. It's not only my safety at stake here, but Mandy's too.

"I'll tell you if I receive another threat. I promise."

# CHAPTER 24

## SAYLOR

A week goes by and Oliver and I are still not talking. He hasn't apologized for what he did. He hasn't said anything to me actually. I can't decide what I'm mostly angry about, being followed by a fucking PI or Oliver's insane jealousy. Does he think I would cheat on him with Liv's ex—or with any other guy for that matter? Am I not allowed to have male friends anymore?

For the past seven days, I've locked myself in the studio and by some miracle, I was able to finish the three songs I had been working on. Mercifully, Remi and Sticks were there to help. Usually, it's Tabatha who helps with the creative, but she's still mad at me. If I knew she would try to change my mind at every turn, I wouldn't have told her about the blood clot.

Allan finally booked us recording studio time and we are there for three days. On the first day, we were like kids discovering Christmas for the first time. The excitement was palpable. It's the second day today and the many hours of non-stop hard work is beginning to take a toll on my body. It's a grim realization, the old Saylor wouldn't be feeling so drained.

Each instrument gets recorded separately for every song in a process called multitrack recording and combined later in a mix.

It allows engineers to mold and shape the sound of each instrument independently from the others. I've already recorded the acoustic guitar arrangements for my solo with Oliver and if everything goes as planned, Oliver and I will have studio time together later today. I'm not looking forward to it.

Right now, it's Sticks' turn inside the magical box—the name Remi gave to the recording room and we all adopted. When Sticks does her solo thing, it's impossible not to fall under the spell of her sound. The drums are not the heart of a band for nothing, and she's one of the most talented musicians I've ever seen.

She gets totally in the zone behind the drums and she becomes a different person, a titan among us mere mortals. I'm watching her through the glass when Allan stops next to me.

"She's amazing, isn't she?" he says.

"Yes."

"I can't believe I didn't recognize her at first."

"Don't beat yourself up about it. I don't think she was offended. She did mention she changed a lot since the time you met her."

"Her hair mostly. She used to be blonde." Allan pauses for a moment and I glance at his profile. I sense he has more to say. "Did she ever tell you what she did for me?"

"No. Sticks doesn't talk much about her life."

"I was going through a terrible phase. My stepfather was a jerk and his idea of family time was to constantly criticize me. I was fifteen when Sticks caught me trying to drink an entire bottle of whiskey. I think she was only thirteen back then, a wisp of a girl. She didn't care I was the son of a celebrity, she wasn't intimidated by me. She told me flat out how stupid I was for drowning my sorrows with alcohol. I couldn't believe her gumption. She then convinced me that playing the drums was a better way to forget whatever problems I had. She tried to teach me how to play that night. It was one of the best evenings I spent in that house."

"Did you only hang out once?"

"Yes. I flew back to Nashville the next day and the following year she wasn't there."

Allan doesn't elaborate and I don't ask. His face is serious now and I know when to drop a subject.

We are quiet for ten more minutes or so before Allan speaks again. "Do you think you will be able to record your duet with Oliver today?"

My spine goes taut as my heart does a painful lurch forward. I was purposely shoving that problem aside and trying not to obsess about it too much. Our duet song is filled with angst and feelings. It demands to be sung with our entire hearts in it.

"I'll try my best."

"That song is a winner, Saylor. It has the potential to take you to the top quicker than you can imagine."

I take a deep breath and try to find the strength to forgive Oliver, even if he hasn't asked for it. In the grand scheme of things, I don't have time to be mad at him. Holding grudges is for those without a quickly approaching expiration date.

Oliver never shows up and Allan can't get a hold of him. My good will toward the man vanishes. I'm tired, cranky, and we wasted hours waiting for the douche canoe to grace us with his presence. Allan decides to call it a day just before Charlotte comes into the studio. I don't like the look on her face.

"Is Oliver here?" She seems flustered as her gaze skates around.

"No. He never showed up," Allan replies.

"Shit."

"What's going on, Charlotte?"

"Today is not a good day for Ollie."

"What do you mean?" I ask.

She turns to me and her eyes soften a bit. "I shouldn't be the one to tell you, but hell. I'm worried about him."

"You're freaking me out. Spill it already," I say through clenched teeth.

"Today would be our brother Harry's nineteenth birthday. He died when he was six years old. Ollie blames himself for it and he never handles this date well. Since you two are still at odds, I know this year will be especially bad."

I don't think Charlotte is trying to make me feel guilty, but the feeling takes hold all the same. "What can I do to help?"

"We need to find him. Any idea where he could be?"

I shake my head, unable to voice out loud I have no idea of Oliver's whereabouts.

"I'll call all his party friends. I know it's a long shot, but I would check the bars and pubs in the area as well."

I make a beeline for my purse on a table nearby. "I'll do it. Have you talked to Sebastian?"

"He's next on my list."

I head out of the studio without saying goodbye to the girls. Worry for Oliver gives me a bout of energy and the previous fatigue is forgotten. My heart is lodged in my throat and my mind is a mess. Why did he never me tell about his brother?

I have no clue where he could be. I don't know any of his favorite spots and what does that tell me about our relationship? I love a man I don't even know. The only place I can think of is the little café he brought me to once, but I doubt he will be there right now. They don't serve alcohol. Instead, I head to Hermosa's Beach main hub by the shore where the majority of bars are concentrated. It's happy hour and the plaza is packed. I'm going on blind hope Oliver is in one of those bars. If he decided to party in L.A., I will never find him.

My feet drag me toward Closing Time. It's not the wildest place in town, but it serves the best beer. Plus, there's a weird tug in my chest, pulling me toward Rori's establishment. I venture in and my heart sinks. The place is full to capacity. My eyes do a quick scan of the room before I search for Rori behind the bar. He's not there. Damn it. I could have used his help.

I realize I'm blocking the entrance when someone touches my shoulder. I walk to the side to allow the couple to enter. *You won't find anything if you don't start to look, Saylor.* I force myself to walk between the tables. Oliver won't be sitting with a large group of people, maybe he'll be in a secluded corner with a bimbo on his lap. The bitter thought makes my heart clench painfully in my chest. Oliver wouldn't do that, would he? Ugh! Why am I having these insecure thoughts?

But the fear that I will find Oliver with another woman is real. It makes my ears ring and my heart rate to spike up in jealousy. I head toward the back of the room where there are few booths that offer more privacy. The occupant of one of them is being blocked by the waitress, who's leaning forward for no good reason, unless she wants to show whoever is sitting there a clear view of her cleavage.

She steps back and turns, and I see a hunched figure with a baseball cap on sitting at the table. His head is dipped low and in front of him there's a glass, and a half empty bottle of whiskey. I quicken my steps and reach the table before the waitress has the chance to leave. She narrows her eyes at me.

"He doesn't want to be bothered," she says with a tone of possession. I don't know her. She must be new.

"Then fucking leave already," I say.

Her jaw drops at the same time her eyes flash with fury. I'm hoping this tramp will say something out of line so I can punch her in the face. I'm dying for a good old cat fight if only to distract me from the turmoil in my head and heart. But Oliver raises his head and says, "Saylor?"

The woman whips her face in his direction. "Do you know her?"

Her incredulous tone almost makes me laugh. "I'm his girl-friend. Now move along."

My reply doesn't please her one bit. When Oliver doesn't deny my claim, she has no choice but to put her tail between her legs and leave.

"How did you find me?" Oliver asks, bringing my attention

back to him. I slide into the booth, but keep a good distance between us.

"You missed your appointment. We're supposed to record our duet today."

Oliver shrugs and pours himself another dose of whiskey. "I didn't think you would want to sing anything with me." He throws his head back and drinks the shot in one single gulp.

"I know how to separate things."

Oliver looks at me, his eyes bloodshot and so fucking sad. "Well, I don't."

Okay, I'm not going anywhere here, so might as well bring the real problem to the surface. "I know what date it is today. Charlotte filled me in."

A myriad of emotions flashes in his eyes. "She had no right."

"Why not? Wasn't Harry her brother, too?"

Oliver grinds his jaw and looks down at his empty glass. "She didn't kill him." His voice is so low I almost don't hear it.

I reach out and touch his hand. My heart is breaking for him. I can't imagine what it must feel like to carry that kind of guilt. It makes my own turmoil pale in comparison. "And what makes you think you did?"

He glances at me again and the sadness I read on his expression leaves me raw. It makes me want to hold him tight and never let go.

"I was the one who told him to get lost. He's dead because I was too embarrassed to be around him and I sent him away."

"You were a child."

"It doesn't matter!" He slams his open palm against the wooden table, rattling the empty glass and the bottle. "My age at the time doesn't change the fact if weren't for me, he would still be alive."

I pull back and glare at him. It's obvious that Oliver has taken more than just alcohol to dull his pain. I knew he used recreational drugs in the past, but whether for my sake or not, he toned his nasty habit down around me.

"So you've decided to join him now?" I say, ignoring how hypocritical my statement is.

He rolls his eyes and pours another dose of whiskey into his glass. "Don't be so dramatic."

"You're the one moping in a dark corner of a pub with a bottle of whiskey, and you call me dramatic?"

"Why are you here, Saylor? I thought you were done with me."

His question takes me by surprise. "You thought we were through?"

"Isn't that your MO? Walk away without ending things properly?" He raises an eyebrow at me while his lips curl into an ugly grin.

His words feel like a punch to my stomach and I can't fault him for thinking like that.

"I was mad at you. I still am. You never apologized for invading my privacy."

"You're not going to get an apology. I'm not sorry for what I did. I was trying to protect you. I won't let another person I love die without doing anything to prevent it."

*Go ahead, Oliver, keep striking at my heart.* Not that he has any idea how his words are gutting me right now.

"And demanding to know what I was doing with Derek is protecting my life how?"

"I was jealous. That wanker almost ruined my best mate's wedding."

"Oh my God. Get over it. Derek is a friend." I grab the bottle of whiskey and bring it to my lips, taking large sips from it.

"Whoa, what are you doing?"

I don't stop until the alcohol begins to work and my body relaxes. I wipe my lips with the back of my hand and place the bottle down with a resounding thud. "I need alcohol if I'm to sit here and listen to you without smacking you upside the head."

His jaw drops before his eyes turn to slits. "Do you love me?"

"What kind of question is that? I'm here aren't I?"

"Stop evading and answer the question, Saylor. Do you love me or not?"

"Yes. I love you, you idiot."

He slides closer until his leg touches mine. His arm snakes around my waist, trapping me against his body as his face stops inches from mine. "Good, because I'm about to fuck your mouth."

He doesn't wait for my response and crushes his lips against mine, his whiskey flavored tongue prying my mouth open almost cruelly. I don't offer resistance. Instead, I give back to him in the same savage manner, biting his lower lip to show Oliver he's not in total control here. His free hand finds its way between my legs, the skirt I'm wearing offering no barrier against his probing fingers. He pushes my panties out of the way and inserts two fingers inside my already soaked pussy. I don't care we are in a crowed pub, that anyone looking in our direction will see Oliver and me in a full-on foreplay session. I didn't know how starved I was for this infuriating man until I tasted him again.

The sound of glass shattering nearby manages to break through my lust infused brain and I pull away.

"We can't do this here. Someone might see us."

"Sugar, I don't give a damn." He leans closer again but I place both hands against his chest and push him back.

"I do." I grab his wrist and stop his fingers from fucking me. My core is throbbing and I'm not far away from a shattering orgasm, but I don't want it to happen here, in public. That would cheapen the moment. I slide away from him and try to fix my skirt in the process.

"Are you leaving me?" Oliver's expression is pitiful to the point of being comical.

"No, I'm taking you away." I pull my wallet out of my purse and grab all the cash I have in it, dropping it on the table for effect. I hope it's enough to cover Oliver's tab. "Come on. Time is wasting."

I turn and begin to walk away, fighting not to look back to see if Oliver is following me. I don't know what will be my next move if he decides to stay. Dragging him out by his short hair is not something I want to do. But he does follow me and wraps his arm around my waist in a possessive way, making it hard to walk between the tables.

Once outside the crowded pub, I pry Oliver's arm from around me and hold his hand instead, lacing our fingers together. He stares at our fused hands for one second before looking up again. I know he wants to pull me closer for a kiss. I would have let him do it if I didn't have other ideas. I tug at his hand. "Come. There's a place I want to show you."

# CHAPTER 25
## SAYLOR

drive to a spot I haven't been to since I was a happy teen, aka, before the attack. It's already past nine and Littleton's most famous antique store is closed. I park in front of the darkened building and get out of the vehicle. The street is deserted at this hour—the store is off Littleton's main commercial track.

"Where are we?" Oliver stares at the closed shop before his eyes do a quick perimeter check of the area.

"Follow me."

I walk past the front door and turn the corner onto a one-way street. Blueberries' Antiques looks small at first, but once you walk around the building and reach the back, you can see the store's big open lot filled with treasures to be discovered. A wired fence keeps intruders out, or at least tries to. It never deterred me. I'm happy to see that the big tree against the barrier is still there. It has grown taller since the last time I was here but it's still climbable.

I come closer and touch the bark with my open palm. "Hello, old friend."

"You know you are talking to a tree, right?"

I look over my shoulder. "Marvin and I go way back."

"It has a name?" Oliver shakes his head and grins. "Of course it does."

He moves closer and even in the darkness, I can read Oliver's intentions in his eyes. I put my hands up. "I didn't bring you here so you could fuck me against a tree in the middle of the street."

Oliver takes advantage that my back is almost flush against the tree trunk, places his hands on each side of my head, and leans forward, caging me in. "Don't tell me the idea doesn't make your pussy soaking wet for me."

"Let me make this very clear to you. We're not fucking in public."

Oliver looks left and right. "There's no one around."

I give him a light shove. "Stop being a perv and help me climb up."

He pouts, making him look adorable, but I don't act on the impulse to kiss him. That would only lead to trouble. Oliver finally decides to get with the program, and gives me a boost so I can reach the lower branch of the tree. From there, it's easy to make progress up.

"So, you don't want to make sweet love to me in public but you want to commit a crime instead."

"Shh, stop talking and follow me."

Perched on the second highest branch, I can reach the top of the fence easily. I swing one leg over, holding onto it, then the other follows, before I let go and fall to the other side in a crouch. Oliver is still standing frozen next to Marvin.

"What are you waiting for? Can't climb a tree?"

"You're mental, you know that?"

I cross my arms in front of my chest and smirk. "Oh my, it looks like someone is scared."

He rolls his eyes. "Please."

Oliver grabs the branch I had been too short to reach without assistance, and brings his lean body up. With the grace of a cat, he works his way up and jumps the fence. It only takes him a few seconds.

He drops in front of me with an eat-shit grin on his face. "You were saying?"

"Show off." I turn on my heel and walk away. He follows me.

"So, what's this place?"

"If you haven't guessed it by now, this is an antique and second-hand shop."

"It looks like a place where old furniture comes to die. I only see junk."

I ignore his jab and keep walking between the stacked pieces of patio furniture and other outdoor things that have seen better days.

"I used to come here all the time when I was younger. My mother and I loved to find hidden gems for our DIY projects. I pretended this back lot was an island filled with treasure chests, waiting for me to find them. This wreckage is what inspired the name of the band."

Oliver keeps following me without saying much. He stops from time to time to inspect something that catches his eye, but I keep on walking until I find the old and rusty swing I was hoping would still be here. It's in the same spot as before, and does it make me weird that I get overly emotional over such an ugly thing? It's in worse condition than I remember. One of the swing chains is broken and the seat is barely hanging there, dangling in an angle, waiting for death. Just like me. I touch the remaining chain and give it a pull. It creaks, but stays strong. This one is not ready to give up yet. I can't help but think that this is a sign somehow.

I feel a warm touch on my shoulder and look over at the man behind me. I didn't even hear him approach.

"Why did you bring me here, sugar?" His voice is softer, almost a whisper.

"Today, when Charlotte came looking for you, I realized that I know nothing about you. What are your likes and dislikes?

What are your favorite places to hang out? I don't even know what your favorite food is. And then it occurred to me you also don't know much about me." I pause and let my gaze take in the darkened lot. "So I figured, I should show you this place."

Oliver wraps his arms around my waist, hugging me from behind, and rests his chin on my shoulder. "I love football, the original kind. I hate the feel of wet sand under my feet, and my favorite place to hang out is anywhere I can see the open sky."

I twist in his arms so I can look at his face. "And favorite food?"

His lips curl into a devilish grin. "Your pussy."

I pinch his arm. "You're terrible."

The smile vanishes from Oliver's face and his eyes turn serious. "I'm sorry I've been such a jackass. I love you so much that the thought of something happening to you drives me out of my mind. I can't think straight."

My breathing stops and my heart clenches painfully inside my chest. He's going to hate me when this is all said and done. I rise on the tip of my toes and kiss him so he can't see the guilt in my eyes. It's a sweet kiss but with enough heat to make my stomach flutter. We both try to keep our desires contained, bottled in until we can take this further in a better setting. It's almost like we are teenagers, content to only explore each other's mouth.

A dog barks nearby and we jump apart. Not even a foot from us, we can see the silhouette of a big German Shepherd.

"You didn't say they had a watch dog." Oliver tries to push me behind him. The dog barks and growls, inching forward. "Okay, you run to the fence while I distract the beast."

I narrow my eyes at the approaching animal and I can't believe what I'm seeing. "Xander?"

The German Shepherd angles his head to the side, before breaking into a run in our direction.

"Fuck. Run, Saylor!"

I walk away from Oliver's body shield and crouch to receive

the dog's hug and kiss. "I can't believe you're still alive," I say between giggles.

"Let me guess, old friends?" Oliver says from behind me.

"Yes, I've known Xander since he was a puppy." I stand up and the dog keeps dancing around me.

"Blimey, I thought we were toast."

Xander decides to pay attention to Oliver and growls in his direction.

"Okay, maybe I'm still toast."

"Down boy, Ollie is a friend." I pat the dog's head.

Xander proceeds to sniff Oliver until he deems him nonthreatening. Then he walks a few paces to the side and lays down on his furry belly.

"Harry always wanted a dog," Oliver says almost absent-mindedly.

"And you didn't?"

Oliver shrugs and looks out into the distance. "Sure. Dogs are great. But Harry was obsessed about the idea. He used to ask for one every day, he'd buy dog training magazines with his allowance and leave them all around the house. It drove our mother bonkers."

"She never caved in?"

Oliver shakes his head. "No. My parents aren't animal lovers."

There are so many questions I want to ask, but I'm afraid to.

"We couldn't afford a dog, but Mom got me a goldfish once. It died two weeks later."

"Jeez, what happened?"

"Dunno. One day I came back from school, went to check on Elvis, and there he was, floating belly up."

"You didn't forget to feed him, did you?" Oliver smirks at me.

I swat at his arm. "No, jerk. I was a responsible kid."

He grabs my hand and pulls me into an embrace. "You must

have been such an adorable little girl. I would love to see pictures."

I take a step back and put some distance between us. All my childhood pictures are at my mother's place and I'm not ready to go there. This trip down memory lane has lasted long enough and I'm ready to return to the present.

"Come on, let's go. I'm hungry."

"For me, I hope."

Feeling naughty, I give him a come-hither look. "I'm always hungry for you, babe."

# CHAPTER 26
## TAYLOR

I drive us back to my place because for once, I don't want to be awakened by the sound of Allan coming into the office. Oliver's idea to run his business from home is becoming more and more inconvenient. I keep my opinion to myself, though.

Once I park in front of the Goulas residence, Oliver peers out the window. "Are you sure this is okay?"

His question is not unusual. This is the first time I've brought him here. In reality, he has never set foot in my house. But if I'm going to let him into my life for real, I might as well start with the place I call home.

"Yes, as long as we keep quiet."

Oliver turns to me with a grin on his lips and with eyes that sparkle with mischief. "This feels so high school, sneaking into your bedroom when everybody is asleep. I wonder if I'll get lucky tonight."

"If you play your cards right," I tease and Oliver narrows his eyes, the amusement in his gaze turning into heat in a split second.

"Oh, sugar. I plan to." He runs his fingers down my arm in a feather light touch, leaving a trail of goose bumps in its path. I shiver and rub my legs together before getting out of the car.

The chilly night air does nothing to cool off my feverish skin. Oliver follows me, and we walk in silence down the path that leads to the small guest house I call home. The only source of illumination comes from the lit up swimming pool and Oliver's gaze is drawn to it.

"Don't even think about it. Remi's parents room faces the pool. I'm not skinny dipping with you."

"I said nothing." Oliver fakes innocence.

Out of habit, I turn the door knob, but find the door locked. I curse under my breath and look for my heavy keychain. I used to keep my door unlocked all the time, but thanks to that stupid note, I started using the key to the guest house Mrs. Ogata gave me when I moved in. Despite my belief the note was just an idiotic prank, I'm still taking precautions.

The door creaks loudly when I open it. Funny how I never noticed it before. I turn on the light and Oliver follows me. For once, the place looks tidy. Oliver walks in slowly, taking his time to get a feel of the room before he turns to me.

"Cozy." I don't miss the sarcastic tone in his voice.

I roll my eyes. "Go ahead. You can say it's crap. I don't care."

Most of the furniture is mismatched and old. I haven't bothered refurbishing it. My DIY days are over.

"Where's the bedroom? It has a bed, right?" The corner of his lips twitch upward.

"Shut up. Of course I own a bed."

Oliver moves closer and pulls me flush against his body. "Relax, sugar. I'm only teasing." He kisses the tip of my nose. "Lead the way, please."

I lace my fingers with his and together we walk in my bedroom's direction. I stop in front of the closed door and spare a moment to glance at him. He squeezes my hand and I don't know what to make of that little action on his part. The only thing I know is that my heart is galloping out of control right now. I'm not sure why I feel so nervous all of the sudden. I finally open the door and he follows me in.

I keep my back to Oliver and stare at my unmade bed—shit, he's going to think I'm a slob. I forget my insecure thoughts completely when I feel the heat of his body at my back. He touches my neck, then slides his fingers down my shoulders, eliciting a shiver from me. He tilts my head to the side and places a hot kiss on the base of my neck. I melt into him. His hands glide down my body and when his fingers brush against the underside of my breasts, I stop breathing. He chuckles against my neck, a throaty and sexy sound.

He wraps his arms around my waist and brings his lips to my ear, only to whisper my name. That whisper alone almost makes me come on the spot. I turn in his arms and bring my lips to his. This kiss is different than all the others, it's hungry, passionate, but at the same time, sweet and meaningful. I can taste the heartache, the turmoil, all the emotions bouncing between us.

I jump on his arms and he catches me with ease, his capable hands squeezing my butt cheeks in the process. Our kiss intensifies, it's all tongue and teeth now. We fall onto the bed together, Oliver on top of me, between my legs. My body hums at his touch, my entire skin reacts to him. Then the most shattering orgasm hits out of the blue by the mere friction of his erection against my core. I scream his name as my nails dig into his arms.

"Fuck, sugar. Did you just come?" Oliver looks down at me wide eyed.

I'm still riding the wave of pleasure, so I just close my eyes and nod.

"I knew I was good, but not that good."

My eyes fly open to find Oliver grinning from ear to ear. I watch him through slits before I roll us over in a swift move. Now I'm striding him.

"That didn't count. It has been a week."

Oliver's hands crawl up my thighs until they reach my

panties. His fingers trace the edges of my underwear, making my core throb even more.

"Too fucking long without tasting you," he says but it sounds more like a grunt.

"And whose fault is that?" I raise an eyebrow at him.

"Mine. It's my bloody fault." His thumb swipes against my clit and I fight to suppress a moan. "I promise to not act like a caveman if you promise not to hide stuff from me."

I can't make that promise, but another swipe of his thumb has me mumbling something that sounds like an affirmation.

I'm going to Hell for this.

# CHAPTER 27
## SAYLOR

We recorded our duet the day after Harry's birthday and it was as gut wrenching as I thought it would be. Our song is emotional and beautiful. I only realized it was about us in the moment I found myself alone with Oliver in the 'magical box', cut off from the world. We wrote a song about our love without even knowing.

*Will Oliver be able to listen to it once I'm gone without feeling betrayed?*

Thoughts like this have being plaguing my mind more frequently. Doubt has crept into my brain and my heart. I keep hearing Tabatha's and Derek's pleas, and the underlying accusations—*Why are you such a coward, Saylor?*

I've lost count of how many times my finger hovered over Derek's contact number. But I always end up chickening out and not calling him.

To compensate, I put everything I have into work and before I know it, the week passes and our first single is released. It does well, but we are still unknown. It's not until a month later—a week before Thanksgiving Day—when we drop my duet with Oliver that things explode. *Everything & Nothing* manages to crawl up to top 20 in the Billboard charts within a couple of days, and the simple video clip we've put together has over one million views already on YouTube. Wreck of the Day is finally on the map and I have Oliver to thank for it.

I should be happy things are progressing well and as I hoped, but time is going by too fast and the thought that next year I might not be here anymore makes me feel hollow, joyless. I couldn't sleep last night, and I was glad Oliver drank himself to a total stupor celebrating our duet's success, and didn't notice my constant toss and turning. After one round of mind blowing sex, he pretty much passed out.

I get out of bed a little bit before five in the morning, knowing sleep is not going to happen for me. The house is as silent as a tomb, but the vestiges of last night's celebratory dinner party are still visible in the empty champagne bottles and dirty glasses scattered over every surface. I head toward the sliding doors and step outside, welcoming the cold November night air. A frigid breeze comes out of nowhere, turning my skin into ice and almost making me go back inside. I spot a chenille blanket on one of the chaise lounges and make a beeline for it. I sit down and throw the soft protection over my shoulders. I'm still not as toasty as I would have preferred, but I can't bear to go inside the house now. I need the solitude and staring at the illuminated pool has a soothing effect.

Today is Thanksgiving Day and Oliver and I have been invited to celebrate it at Liv's parents. I don't expect to see Mom there, even though Mrs. Dawson always invites her. She probably got a shift at the hospital, something she's been doing for the past few years to avoid every single family-oriented holiday. I wish I could avoid it this year, too. I'm not sure how I'm going to hide the darkness festering inside my chest, the all-consuming guilt.

♡ ♡ ♡

I must have fallen asleep eventually because I wake with someone shaking my shoulder. I blink my eyes open and notice the sun is already up. Charlotte is the one who found me, and now she's sitting on the chair next to mine, staring at me with a question mark in her gaze.

"Let me guess. Couldn't take my brother's snoring any longer?"

"What? No. I just couldn't fall asleep."

"Yes, sometimes alcohol does that to me. I think we all indulged a little bit too much last night. Thank God that's all Ollie did."

She leans back on the chair to stare at the pool and crosses her legs at the ankles.

"You're referring to his drugs consumption, aren't you?"

"Yes. It used to be really bad. It's a miracle he hasn't become a hopeless addict." She turns her face in my direction. "I haven't seen him high since you got together. You're good for my brother."

I avoid her gaze and let her words consume my thoughts. Oliver did get high once since we became a couple on the day of Harry's birthday. We were at odds and that was a rough day. He hasn't touched any drugs ever since. I'd like to think that his dedication to work is what is keeping him from going down that path, not me. I'm actually praying it's not me, because what's going to happen to Oliver and his sanity when I die? Will he throw everything he accomplished away and return to his party-until-you-drop lifestyle?

"I didn't say that to put any pressure on you." Charlotte's voice brings me back from my reverie. "No one should feel responsible for another person's decisions. If you decided to leave my brother and he returns to his nasty habits, that's on him, not you."

"Do you think I'm going to dump Oliver?" I throw my legs to the side of the chair and face Charlotte.

She turns her body in my direction so now our gazes are locked. "Not at this very moment. But people change with time. It could happen. Actually, it will probably happen."

"Have you always had that pessimistic view about love?"

Charlotte shakes her head and smiles without joy. "I'm not pessimistic. I'm realistic."

The last thing I want is to sit here and chat with Charlotte about how she thinks Oliver and I are doomed. I already know we are and it's not for the reasons she's thinking, but I don't need the bitter reminder.

"I'd better get back inside and make some coffee." I stand up. "We have a long day ahead of us."

# CHAPTER 28
## OLIVER

As we drive from Hermosa Beach to Littleton, I try to keep the Cheshire cat grin in check. Saylor has no idea about the surprise we have planned for her. The little rascal never told me her birthday was two days after Thanksgiving Day and if it weren't for Liv wanting to throw Saylor a surprise birthday party, I would still be in the dark. But that's okay. I can't wait to see her reaction when my present is delivered to the Dawson's house later today.

This won't be my first Thanksgiving dinner. Sebastian's uncle used to have those back in London and I've been invited a few times. I have the feeling this will be a completely different experience, though.

I glance at Saylor who is looking out the window, distracted. She's been acting strangely since she awakened. I tried to get her to open up, only to have her claim she was tired. I've caught her rubbing her forehead a couple of times, as if she was trying to massage away a brewing headache. She could be hungover, even though I don't remember her drinking that much last night.

I felt better when she presented me her clean bill of health. I didn't even bother reading it. So I stopped looking for signs that Saylor isn't one hundred percent well, but today it's impossible not to see that something is up with her. I don't bloody understand why she's so closed off sometimes. Despite the promise we made to each other to be honest, I know she's not keeping her end of the bargain. She's hiding something from me.

I turn onto the Dawson's street and force my mood killer thoughts to a dark corner. I can't obsess about them now. It's time to put on the Oliver Best charm. I spot Sebastian's car right away parked on the driveway and a few others.

We find the door unlocked and Saylor calls out Liv's mom's name as she steps into the entry foyer. We hear a reply from the kitchen and that's where we head, Saylor holding the boxes of pie, and me bringing the container of booze.

Everyone seems to be in the big open kitchen, including Liv's sister and her husband. Kimmy's stare zeroes in on the box in my hands and she narrows her eyes. "Did you bring enough booze to get a college town drunk?"

I look down and count the bottles of whiskey, tequila, and gin. Maybe I did go overboard. I didn't know what everyone liked to drink, so I got everything. "Maybe."

Owen, Kimmy's husband, walks around her and takes the box from my hands, placing it on the kitchen island. "Not bad, not bad at all."

"I thought you were a beer guy."

"Not when I have this." He pulls the bottle of Hendrick's gin from the box. "Hey, Murphy, we got tonic, right?"

"Yes, it should be in the garage with everything else."

"Coolio." Owen makes a start in the direction of the garage door, but Kimmy puts a hand on his arm.

"You're not going to start drinking now, are you? You have work to do."

"Chillax, babe. I'm just going to put the soda in the fridge."

"And you need the bottle of gin to do it?" She arches an eyebrow at him.

Owen lets out a sigh of defeat and puts the bottle back in the box. He stares at me. "So close."

"Not even," Kimmy replies.

Watching their banter makes something warm and fuzzy spread over my chest. I glance in Saylor's direction. She is distracted playing with Liv's niece. Saylor is smiling and making faces at the baby, much to the kid's delight. I feel a clap on my shoulder and get jolted on the spot.

"Planning to have one of those any time soon?" Bas says.

"Are you fuc—are you mental?"

"Sorry, mate. I couldn't resist. You had this daydream look on your face. It was priceless."

"I'm too young to be a dad." I start to take the bottles of liquor out. "Don't tell me you're trying already."

"Nah. Not that it wouldn't be awesome, but Liv and I need to figure some stuff out first," Bas says that under his breath, as if he doesn't want anyone else to hear him.

I watch him closely. "Is everything alright?"

"Yes, of course." He doesn't hold my gaze so I know he's lying. I won't pester him today, though. It's not the place.

Liv's mom divides all the tasks and that keeps me occupied for the next hour. Then we head outside where Murphy has brought out a big flat TV screen and whoever is not helping in the kitchen is out watching football until it's time for dinner.

During one of the commercial breaks, I turn to Bas. "Is Saylor's mom coming?"

My friend clenches his jaw before answering. "No. She claimed she couldn't switch her shift. That's a bunch of baloney if you ask me."

Bas is pissed and I share the sentiment. Saylor's mother sounds like a winner. Her boyfriend attacks her daughter and in turn she shuts her out. Couldn't even bother to come to Saylor's surprise birthday party. Saylor comes out in that moment to announce dinner will be ready soon and we should head back inside. Chairs shift as everyone begins to get up. I remain on my spot and she comes in my direction, stopping right in front of me.

"Not hungry?"

I wrap my arms around her waist and pull her close, kissing her belly before leaning my cheek on it.

"Yes." I hug her tighter.

She runs her fingers through my hair. "Ollie, what's the matter?"

"Nothing. I just wanted to squeeze you." I look up and stare into her puzzled eyes. "I love you so damn much, Saylor."

Her breath catches and a myriad of emotions flashes in her eyes right before she leans down and kisses me. I taste her for as long as she lets me which is not nearly enough. She pulls back and smiles. "Come on. The food is getting cold."

I let her drag me back inside and everyone has already taken their seats by the long table in the living room. The food has been served and Liv's dad is standing with a fork and knife in each hand, poised to start carving up the turkey.

"Ha, we found the missing ones. Did you get lost on the thirty second walk from the backyard to here?" He looks in our direction with a smirk.

"Something like that," I say and Saylor pinches my butt.

"Right. Let me warn you, the second floor is off-limits to you two. I don't want any shenanigans."

Owen snorts and Murphy turns in his direction. "That includes you too, son. The only person getting lucky in this house tonight is me." He winks at his wife.

"Yew! Dad. Come on. Don't make me puke on my plate," Liv's younger brother says.

I lean closer to Saylor and whisper in her ear, "No wonder you loved to hang out here so much."

She turns her face in my direction, bringing her plump lips close to mine. "Yes, the Dawsons are the best."

I'm a half second from kissing her again when I'm hit on the forehead by a piece of bread. "Dude, no making out at the table either. This is a family celebration." Owen is grinning at me from the other side of the table.

I'm itching to give a smart ass reply, but Saylor squeezes my thigh as a sign for me to keep quiet. She already knows me too well. To tease her, I grab her hand and place it over my crotch so she can feel my already growing erection. She pulls her hand away and glares at me. I just smile from ear to ear.

After everyone has their plates full, Liv's mom says a prayer and we dive in. The food is out of this world and I eat until I can't shove any more of it inside. When all of the plates are empty, comes the best part of dinner.

# CHAPTER 29

## SAYLOR

'm stuffed and if I don't get any caffeine into my body pronto, I will fall into a food induced coma. I help clear the plates and then we bring the pies to the table. I made apple and cherry pie, but I'm really dying to eat Karen's pecan pie. It's what I live for the entire year and she usually makes an extra one for me to bring home. Liv's mom is the best.

Before anyone can dive into the sugary treats, Liv speaks up. "I think each of us should say one thing they are grateful for this year. I'll start." She smiles at Sebastian before glancing at me. "I'm grateful I could have my best friend with me when I married the love of my life."

*What?* I so did not see Liv saying that. "Thank you, Blue, for being part of that wonderful day, for helping me when I needed it the most."

My face is on fire and I don't want know what to say. Next to me, Oliver shifts on his seat before grabbing my hand under the table to squeeze it lightly. I glance at him and there's a twinkle of mischief in his gaze matching the upturn of his lips. Sebastian goes next.

"I'm thankful I have someone in my corner who is not afraid to tell me like it is." Sebastian's gaze turns to Oliver.

"No mate, I'm not talking about you, but you couldn't have picked a better match." Bas glances at me. "Thanks, Blue, for knowing exactly what to say when I was too stupid to see the truth."

My throat begins to burn and my vision gets progressively blurrier. If this continues, I won't be able to keep the wave of swirling emotion from crashing through the protective wall around my heart. I can feel the crack there getting bigger and bigger.

"Okay, okay. My turn," Jeremy says and sits up straighter on his chair. "I'm going to say something here that I probably shouldn't, but since we're doing this, I might as well go for it. Thank you, Saylor, for never saying anything or treating me like an idiot when you found out I had a crush on you."

My jaw drops and I feel heat spreading through my cheeks.

"Wait? You had a crush on Saylor?" Liv turns to her brother. "When?"

Oliver shifts his body and angles it forward, suddenly very interested in Jeremy's answer. Liv's brother senses the change in him and is quick to answer.

"Chill out, dude, *had* a crush, as in past tense."

Oliver only narrows his eyes at Jeremy, but mercifully, doesn't say a thing.

"When I was younger and didn't know better Blue was totally out of my league." Jeremy turns to Oliver and smirks. "She's out of your league too, buddy, so you'd better not fuck it up."

"Jeremy! Language." Karen frowns at her son.

Shit, what are the Dawsons doing to me? The trend continues and everyone at the table says something that I did for them, or shares a story about me. I can barely breathe properly when Oliver's turn comes.

"So, I guess we saved the best for last." He gives me a cheeky smile. "I'm thankful that you gave me such a hard time when we met, that your loyalty for your best friend brought you into my path again, but mostly, I'm thankful you allow me to love you, sugar."

My heart is hammering like mad inside my ribcage and the lump in my throat feels like it's going to crash my windpipe at any minute. It's a miracle no tears have rolled down my cheeks yet. Oliver looks over my shoulder and I turn in time to see Liv's mom come out of the kitchen holding a cake with candles on it. On cue, everyone starts to sing happy birthday to me. I'm in such shock, I just sit there, frozen on the spot. The cake is placed in front of me, and Karen urges me to make a wish and blow out the candles. There's only one thing I want and it's what I ask for even though it's childish to even entertain the idea.

*Time.* I want more time.

Oliver pulls me into a hug and whispers in my ear, "Happy birthday, sugar."

Everyone is talking all at once but I can't hear a thing over the loud buzz in my ears. I begin to feel dizzy. Suddenly, Oliver is pulling me with him toward the front door and out the house. Parked by the curb right in front of the Dawson's, there's a white Range Rover SUV with a big red bow on top.

"What's this?" I ask.

"What do you think? Your birthday gift of course."

"You got me a car?"

"Not any car. A Range Rover, you know, because it's British and I wouldn't have you drive anything else."

I'm shaking my head as I walk toward the beauty. "Ollie, this is too much. I can't accept it."

He stops me in my tracks and spins me around so I'm facing him. "Sugar, this is nothing compared to what I want you to have. You give me so much every day and you have no bloody idea. You deserve the world."

"You shouldn't have," my voice comes out choked and finally the tears I have been holding back begin to fall.

"Why are you crying?" He wipes the wetness from my cheeks.

How can I tell Oliver I'm crying because most likely this is the last birthday I get to celebrate with him? How can I tell him I'm a lying bitch? I step away from his embrace, feeling cold and forlorn in an instant.

"Saylor?" He frowns in my direction, probably wondering why I'm acting this way.

I don't answer him and bolt back to the house, shoving aside whoever was in my way. I run up the stairs and close myself in Liv's old room. I'm making a spectacle out of myself, but it's better than let them see me lose my shit. The sobs come strong and ugly as vicious tears seem to rip at my soul. A few minutes later, I hear footsteps coming up the stairs, and then Liv's mom opens the door.

"Sweetheart, is everything okay?"

Her concerned voice makes me cry harder, so I grab one of the pillows and hide my face in it. She comes into the room and closes the door behind her. A second later, she's sitting next to me on the bed.

"You didn't like the surprise?"

"No. I love it. That's the problem."

"I don't understand."

I look up and I don't know what makes me do it, but I find myself telling Karen the ugly truth that's been crushing my chest. I tell her I'm dying and I've been lying to all of them. I confess something I should be saying to my mother, but in a sense Liv's mom is like a mother to me. She listens to my outpour without interrupting once. When I'm done and feel utterly and completely spent, she pulls my head into her lap and runs her fingers through my hair as if I were a little girl.

"Oh, honey. You shouldn't have carried this burden all alone."

"You're not mad at me?"

"Of course not. I'm sad, so very sad. I love you as much as I love my own kids. I don't like to see you like this, defeated, broken."

I close my eyes. "I'm so scared."

"It's okay to be scared. It's better than being fearless."

"But I'm a coward. I'm not facing my fears."

"If you feel this way, only you can fix it. I have confidence in you, Saylor. You have strength in your heart. You can conquer anything."

I sit up and look at her kind face. "Will you help me?"

"Of course, honey. I'm here for you. I will always be here for you."

I throw myself into her open arms and cry some more. "Please don't tell Liv, yet. I want to do it when I have things figured out."

"I won't. I promise."

Confessing everything to Liv's mom lifted a weight off my chest in a way that telling the truth to Tabatha and Derek didn't. Maybe it's because I'm finally ready to do something about my problems. I'm finally ready to face my demons.

# CHAPTER 30
## SAYLOR

On the evening of my actual birthday, Wreck of the Day will perform live on a televised show. It's our first big public appearance and the girls and I are a bundle of nerves. Everyone is at Renegades HQ bright and early. Well, I spent the night there, something that's now a regular occurrence. Mercifully, Oliver never questioned me about my freak out during Thanksgiving dinner and things sort of resumed to normal. He's giving me space and he'll never know how much that means to me.

Allan is going over the agenda and what we should expect once we get to the venue where the show will take place. Monni will be there to personally assist with our final look for the evening, but he has arranged a courier to deliver our outfits to the house. When the door bell rings, I volunteer to get the package at the door, only to have something to do.

I open the door and find a young UPS guy there with a medium sized box in his hand. I doubt there are any dresses in it. The package is addressed to me, so I sign for it. *Shit*. What if this is a birthday present from Oliver? I don't want to open it in front of everyone, especially if it is another over the top, ridiculously expensive gift. Better open it now, away from the girls' prying eyes.

I rip the tape and part the lid of the box. My blood freezes when I see what's inside. I let out a bloodcurdling scream and let it drop to the floor, jumping backward as the headless rat pops out in all it's gory glory.

I hear hurried footsteps approaching, but I don't turn to see who is coming. My gaze is glued to the dead rodent.

"Saylor, what happened?" Oliver asks right before he spots the box and the rat. "Bloody hell. Who gave this to you?"

"The UPS guy."

Oliver jumps over the box and goes after the man, but the truck has already left. Now, everyone has joined me in front of the house and they are all talking at once.

Oliver returns and pulls me tight against his chest. "Everything is going to be okay, sugar."

"Who sent you this?" Tabatha asks.

"I don't know."

"Is there a note?" Remi takes a step forward.

Allan crouches in front of the open box and pulls an envelope from it. Without asking for my permission, he opens it and reads the note that was inside. His jaw clenches at the same time his grip on the paper seems to tighten.

"What the fuck does it say?" Oliver asks.

Allan looks up with a somber expression on his face, but he doesn't make eye contact with me. "That's your future, bitch."

I swallow hard, the only reaction from me. I feel numb.

"Does it say anything else?" Tabatha pries the note from Allan's hand.

"No. That's it."

"That's awful. We need to call the police," Remi says.

I step out of Oliver's embrace and turn to her, finally snapping out of my stupor. "No! We're not calling the police."

My statement seems to shock the hell out of everyone if I'm

to judge by their facial expressions and the sudden silence that follows.

"You're joking, right? We have to report it," Oliver says, earning a glare from me.

"I'm not calling the police. It's just a stupid prank," I say through clenched teeth and Oliver narrows his eyes at me. I brace myself for an argument of epic proportions.

"I wouldn't categorize that as a simple prank," Sticks puts her two cents in.

I know I'm not going to win anything here, so I march toward the box, kick the rat back inside, before yanking the note from Tabatha's hand and ripping it to shreds.

"I don't want to involve the police, so just drop it, okay?"

Sticks seems to be the only one who gets I have reasons to be acting like a lunatic and she doesn't say another word.

"Destroying evidence doesn't make the threat go away." Oliver stops in front of me, fury sparking in his eyes. He won't let this go.

I walk past him, back into the house. He follows me. I don't stop until I find myself in his bedroom. He comes in and shuts the door with enough force it rattles the picture frames on the wall.

"Stop running away from me. Why don't you want to call the cops? Just tell me the reason, Saylor."

"I can't tell you, so let it drop."

"I thought we had agreed to not keep any secrets from each other anymore."

I did make that promise in a moment where my mind wasn't thinking straight. I knew then it was shallow and meaningless.

"I'm sorry." My reply is so feeble, it might as well have been vapor.

That's clearly not the answer Oliver was hoping for. He clenches his jaw and doesn't hide the tempest brewing in his gaze. He storms out the room without uttering another word.

My stomach bottoms out and my legs can't hold me up right any longer. I sit on the edge of his bed, hide my face between my hands, and crumble like a fucking sand castle.

# CHAPTER 31

## OLIVER

want to break something as I stride out my bedroom and veer to the common area. When I enter the open space, all eyes turn to me.

"Is everything okay?" Allan asks.

"I can't be here." I grab my keys and head to the door.

"We have to be at the L.A. Forum in a couple of hours," he reminds me.

"I'll be there," I grunt not knowing how I'll manage to hop on a stage and sing a love song with Saylor when I want to throttle her.

I have no direction in mind when I rev up the engine of my car and peel out the garage. For the first time since I got trashed on Harry's birthday, I feel the need to dull the anger with drugs. But I don't want to get high out of my mind and ruin the performance tonight. Despite what everyone believes about me, I'm not as reckless as I appear to be. I want Renegades Productions to prosper. It's a matter of pride. I need to prove to myself more than anyone else I can be successful thanks to my brains and hard work and not because of my pretty face.

My phone rings and I almost shut the thing off. I glance at it and see Sebastian's name flashing on the screen. With a click of a button on the steering wheel, his voice comes through the car speakers.

"Speak," I say.

"Hello to you too, mate. What crawled up your ass?"

"Saylor."

Some wanker cuts me off and I press the heel of my hand on the horn.

"She can be difficult. Are you headed to the L.A. Forum already? Liv wants to know what time we should be there, but Saylor is not answering her phone."

"Well, we had a fight."

"Is it serious? Are you breaking up?"

"For fuck's sake, Bas. You sound like a fifteen-year-old girl."

"Piss off."

"I don't know how to do this." My confession comes out in a rushed breath.

"Do what? Be in a relationship?"

"Yes."

"I'm not the best person to seek advice from."

I sense a troubled tone in my friend's voice, but I have my own shit to deal with right now.

"Do you feel like having a drink?"

"It's not even noon yet."

"So what?"

There's a pause and I'm about to tell Bas to forget it, when he finally replies. "Yes, sure. Why the hell not?"

"I'll be at your place in fifteen."

I end the call. It never occurred to me to call Sebastian, but I'm glad it's him I'm meeting. He will keep me in check, and maybe I can get him to give me some pointers about Saylor. What the fuck do I have to do for her to trust me?

♡ ♡ ♡

## SAYLOR

It goes without saying what happened in the morning killed any feeling of euphoria among our group. Tabatha and Remi are also pissed at me for not wanting to report the incident to the police. The only person who seems to understand is Sticks. I have the feeling she also carries a big secret and can relate to my predicament.

Allan doesn't push the police issue, but he does ask a lot of questions which I'm sure he will report back to the PI he hired. I don't have it in me to argue with him about it, at least not today. One particular question that gets stuck with me though is whether I believe my biological father is involved in those threats. I wouldn't be surprised if he was. He's a politician and in my book, they are all rotten.

Monni has made room in his busy schedule to personally take care of our look for the evening. The band is only performing one song, the duet with Oliver, and our stylist decided to put me in a softer, more romantic get up. It's an off-white cropped top that leaves my midriff bare and a high-waist, billowing skirt of the same color with dual front splits that go high up the thighs, showing a lot of leg when I walk. Peach colored highlights were added to my hair which has been styled to perfection with soft curls going down my back. There's nothing rock n' roll chic about my look.

Oliver is making his rounds, talking to people and purposely avoiding me. I try to remain indifferent when women approach him to openly flirt. There's been speculation in the media already about our relationship, but when did that ever deter skanks? I know not all of women who go after Oliver are sluts, but jealousy is running freely through my veins, and I can't help the ugly thoughts popping into my head.

It's not like I'm not receiving male attention on my own end, but I just smile and pretend to be interested in whatever the guys who come to talk to me are saying, just to be polite. I feel numb, not even getting the fangirl feels when artists who I have admired for so long congratulate me for my music.

A guy wearing gigantic headsets on his head and holding an iPad in his hand lets us know we are expected by the stage in five minutes. Oliver materializes next to me, placing a hand on my lower back and leaning down to whisper in my ear.

"Don't be nervous."

I turn to look at him, bringing our lips dangerously close. "I'm not nervous."

Oliver's eyes drop to my mouth and he swallows hard. "Good." He takes a step back, looking at me intensely. I wish I could read his mind.

No time to dwell on it, our time is up. The girls and I take our places on the darkened portion of the stage, just like we rehearsed earlier, while the host says a bunch of gibberish to entertain the audience before introducing us. On cue, the band starts the intro part of the song. I don't have my guitar with me, which makes me feel completely naked. The producers didn't want any type of barrier between Oliver and me. This performance is supposed to be sexy, we're invading each other's space.

I'm afraid my voice will fail me when I sing the first verses alone while the spotlight is on me. But it comes out as it should, and with each verse, I gain confidence. Oliver enters the stage when we come to his part, and the audience goes wild. I glance over my shoulder, giving him a come-hither look. I forget about our fight. I forget we're supposed to be mad at each other. All I feel in this moment is heat, desire, and love, so much love. It's exactly what the song is about. Music can do that, transcend you to a better place.

Oliver stops behind me and curls his arm around my bare stomach, pulling me closer to him. Goose bumps erupt on my skin as he sings close to my ear. I forget there's an audience, that millions of people are watching this on TV. It's only about Oliver and me on the stage right now, how his touch makes my skin burn, how my heart is ready to burst out of my chest.

We sing the final verses looking into each other's eyes, and I pour all of my feelings into those words. I want Oliver to know how much I love him, even if we're done after tonight. My heart is beating at the speed of light and there's a buzz in my ears. The song ends and the audience erupts into applause and whistles, but the world has ceased to exist. It's only Oliver and me.

I'm taken by surprise when his arm snakes around my waist and he pulls me flush against his body for a full on, sexy as hell kiss. We weren't supposed to do this, but hell if I'm going to fight it. The kiss doesn't last more than a few seconds. I bet no one can mistake now that the chemistry, the sparks between Oliver and me, are one hundred percent real.

My face is in flames, but my mortification is meaningless when I read the raw desire in Oliver's eyes and a 'To-Be-Continued' message in his gaze. I'm so ready to get out of here.

# CHAPTER 32
## OLIVER

kissed her on that stage in front of millions and I don't regret one bit of it. Let the world know that Saylor Blue Carter is mine. That outfit Monni picked for her left me in a constant stage of semi-arousal the entire night. On that stage, my erection was full on. Even if the cameras didn't show that to viewers at home, they captured the burning desire on my face, of that I'm sure. Fuck it. Let them see it.

In silent agreement, we leave the premises as soon as we are able to, and I hate we drove in separate cars. My cock is throbbing inside my jeans as I follow Saylor's SUV taillights, wishing she would drive faster. I call her because I need to hear her sexy voice.

"Hey," she says.

"Do you have any idea how much I want you right now?"

"You just called me to say that?" I can hear the smile in her voice.

"My cock is so hard, sugar. I can't wait to plunge it into your sweet pussy." There's a sharp intake of breath on the other side of the line and that brings a grin to my lips. "Tell me how wet you are."

"My panties are soaked." Her voice is raspier than usual and I know desire is doing that. My cock twitches.

"Are you touching yourself, sugar?"

"Yes."

"Fuck." I open my zipper and free my rock hard erection. I need to find some release. "Tell me what you're doing."

"I'm stroking my clit. Hum, I wish it were your fingers gliding down there."

"Soon, sugar, very soon." I begin to pump my cock, spreading pre-cum over its length to make it easier.

"What are you doing, Ollie? Are you being naughty?" Her breathless voice comes through the speakers.

"You bet, sugar. I wish it was your mouth wrapped around my cock instead of my hand."

"Oh, God. I'm coming," she says and that drives me over the edge. I grunt and pump faster, the one hand on the steering wheel having to work extra hard to keep my car inside its lane. I work my cock until I make a mess out of my jeans. Totally worth it, though.

I slow down and take my gaze off the road for a split second to look for tissues. I'm not sure where we are exactly, but I'm glad the road is somewhat devoid of traffic. I snap my attention back to it when I hear a car zap past me. It swerves sharply to the right, hitting Saylor's SUV on the side and pushing it off the road before speeding away.

"What the fuck!"

Saylor's car hits the gravel at full speed and I'm afraid it will spin out of control, but she manages to prevent that somehow, stopping the vehicle at an odd angle a few feet ahead. I hit the brakes and I'm out of my car in the next second while my heart feels like it's going to burst through my chest.

"Saylor!"

The front side of the Range Rover took the brunt of the impact and when I open the driver's door, all I see is the deployed airbag and Saylor's unmoving form.

"No, no, no. Saylor, talk to me."

I push the airbag out of the way and I'm glad to find Saylor's eyes open. She has a gash on her forehead that's bleeding a bit. Her gaze seems confused. I want to run my hands all over her body to make sure she's okay, but I don't know if it's going to do more harm than good.

She turns her face to me slowly with wide eyes. "That car came out of nowhere."

"It pushed you off the road on purpose."

I try to keep my voice low, but the sudden anger pumping in my veins makes it difficult.

"Help me get out of here, please," she says.

I do as she asks, and when she's finally out of the mangled car, I hug her tight. It kills me to feel her body tremble, to see her so shaken up.

"We need to report this, sugar. Enough is enough." Her body tenses up and she pulls back. "Don't try to convince me otherwise, Saylor. That was an attempt on your life."

She steps away from my embrace and walks back to my car, opening the passenger side door and getting in. I follow her, closing the door and turning to look at her. She stares ahead at her wrecked car.

"You can't call the police, Oliver."

"Saylor…"

She turns to me, "You can't call them because I lied."

"What are you talking about?"

"I lied about the attack. I wasn't alone that day. I didn't kill the monster who tried to rape me."

"Who did?" I ask even though I have a feeling I know the answer already.

"Mandy did."

I rub my face with my hand and stare at the road. "You lied to protect her."

"Yes."

"What does that have to do with someone trying to kill you?"

"Remember that first note? It mentions Mandy. I tried to deny it at first. I convinced myself the ginger it was referring to was Connor not Mandy. But it has to be her. Someone out there knows our secret."

"Do you think it could be your father?"

"I don't know. But you see, that's why I can't go to the cops."

I glance at Saylor again. My heart feels as heavy as it did when I was told Harry had died. I couldn't save him, but I will do everything in my power to keep Saylor safe. I reach for the tissue box and slowly, I begin to clean the blood on her forehead.

"Why didn't you tell me this before?"

"I committed a crime, Ollie. I didn't want to turn you into an accomplice."

I stare into her eyes. I see bravery and the fierce will to protect. Saylor is a warrior, an Amazon, and the feeling I'm undeserving of her love comes unbidden. I lean over the console separating us and kiss her as gently as I can, while out of nowhere, my eyes prickle.

She moves closer to me, and if the car wasn't so small, I would pull her across the console completely so she could sit astride me. We make do with what we have and keep exploring each other's mouth as we have never done before, unhurried and reverently.

When we break apart minutes later, I don't try to hide the tears that have rolled down my face. Saylor wipes them off with her thumb without saying a word. I take her hand and kiss her open palm.

"Move in with me."

"What?" Her voice comes out as a squeak and I smile.

"You already spend most of the nights at my place anyway. Let's make it official."

Saylor keeps staring at me without saying a word and my heart takes off. Nervousness makes my mouth go dry. I'm a fucking lost cause when it comes to this woman.

"Okay."

I shake my head because I can't believe my ears.

"Just to clarify. That means, bringing all your stuff to my place, and dealing with my arsehole attitude twenty-four seven."

*Why are you trying to dissuade her from the idea, idiot?*

She smiles. "Yes, I get the gist. You would make a terrible salesperson, you know?"

# CHAPTER 33
## OLIVER

I tell Allan what happened after the show, at least part of it, because he needs to be aware of what's going on. I'm keeping Saylor protected no matter what.

"Let me get this straight. We can't call the cops and you can't tell me the reason. So what am I supposed to do?" He crosses his arms and watches me through slits.

"Get the PI working around the clock. I want to know if Saylor's arsehole father is behind it."

Allan's eyebrows shoot to the heavens. "You truly believe her own father would try to kill her?"

"He's a politician, Allan. Those crooks are capable of anything. He has a lot to lose if his dirty secret comes to the surface."

Allan's gaze turns inward and he nods. "I'll ask my guy to work exclusively on the case."

"Good. I also want to hire security guards, not only for Saylor, but for everyone in the band."

"Did you talk with Saylor about this? Did she agree?" He already knows how stubborn she can be.

"Not yet. But I will."

Definitely not the answer Allan was expecting if the deep

furrow of his eyebrows is any indication. He turns his gaze to the laptop and begins to type away.

"Now that you pulled that stunt during last night's performance, we really can't afford for you and Saylor to fight. Downloads of your single have gone through the roof on iTunes and the gossip sites are having a field day. It was a good marketing move, I gotta say."

"That wasn't a stunt meant for extra publicity," I say through clenched teeth, annoyed that Allan would even imply what I did was for business reasons only.

"Well, it worked out that way. It's all good really. I have received tons of emails and phone calls already. Everybody wants to know more about your relationship with Saylor. My contact at the CW is very interested in featuring a couple of Wreck of the Day's songs in their shows."

I just nod but I'm half listening to Allan. I can't focus on business matters now when I'm still fucking worried about Saylor. Last night, when we got back here, we tried to forget—or put aside temporarily at least—the ugly reality. Saylor's gash turned out to be just a superficial scratch and it didn't warrant a trip to the emergency room. Her wrecked car was a different story, and it took me forever to find a tow truck driver who would collect the vehicle without a police report. But everything has a price and I managed to get a hold of a sketchy character through an old acquaintance who was willing to do the job.

I head back to my bedroom—I guess I should be calling it our bedroom now—and I find her in the same curled up position from when I left her earlier. I close the door behind me with a soft click, but I don't approach the bed, choosing to remain by the door so I can watch her sleep for a little longer. It's funny how life can pull a one-eighty on you within such a short period of time. I could have never imagined that I would care for someone so intensely, so deeply, six months ago. Yet, here I am, ready to lay down my life if it means keeping Saylor safe. I rub my chest when I feel a sudden heaviness there, an ache, just by remembering what could have happened last night. I can't lose Saylor. I will not survive.

♡ ♡ ♡

## SAYLOR

I keep my eyes closed and pretend to be sound asleep, but I can feel Oliver's stare just the same. I heard when he entered the room and closed the door lightly. He hasn't approached the bed and I didn't hear him move, so my guess is he's rooted by the door.

I don't want to announce I'm awake. I don't want to look into his worried gaze. Last night, I saw what my death would mean to him. His eyes had fear in them I've never witnessed from him before.

I can't do that to him. I love him too damn much to give up like a coward. Liv's mom believes in me. It's high time I started believing in myself as well. I have to be brave, I have to face my fears. But he can't see my expression right now. I don't think I can hide what I'm thinking. I might cave in and confess it all. I don't want to worry him even more right now, not before I have a concrete plan in place. I'm calling Derek today and asking for that referral.

I'm Saylor Blue Carter. I've survived every curve ball life has thrown at me, I can conquer this illness as well.

# CHAPTER 34
## SAYLOR

The next day, I tell Mandy about the threatening notes I received and about the dead rat in the box. I have no choice. She promises to be careful, but she doesn't react as badly as I thought she would. Her therapy sessions must be working really well. She has confidence now she didn't before. She doesn't mind the bodyguard either that I asked Oliver to get her.

Life passes in a blur in the next week. No more anonymous letters, no more attempts on my life, but it doesn't mean I'm in the clear. Oliver is ever vigilant, he doesn't let me out of his sight unless Tony, my personal bodyguard, is with me.

Oliver is convinced my father is behind it. If that's the case, it means he has no interest in really harming Mandy. The thought gives me a little peace of mind. It's moronic to think that way, to be relieved my psycho father is the one trying to off me. I take what I can get. It's better the devil you know—kind of—than the one you don't.

Wreck of the Day continues its way to the top. We release another single, a more upbeat song that gets included in the soundtrack of an upcoming teen comedy movie. That solidifies the band's success on its own merit, not on the fact I'm Oliver's girlfriend.

It doesn't mean the media leaves us alone. Paparazzi surge in droves, they all want to snap a picture of Oliver and me together. It's unnerving and intrusive as hell, but Oliver doesn't seem one bit bothered by it. Well, that used to be his life when he was part of Boys Future. He says I'll get used to it. I seriously doubt it. One thing he's right about is with all the attention, it will be harder for someone to do me harm. I guess that's one way to see the glass half full.

Today, I'm nervous for several reasons. I'm going to see Derek's mentor, the brain surgery guru he recommended. I asked him to be present during the appointment, even though I'm risking Oliver getting mad as hell at me when he finds out. That alone would be enough to give me jitters, but I'm mostly nervous because I'll have to lie to Oliver one last time. I'm sure I'll be followed and I wonder what stories the gossip magazines will concoct.

Wreck of the Day also has a beach concert later tonight. Another televised event and I always get extra butterflies in my stomach before a performance.

Oliver brings me breakfast in bed, scrambled eggs and bacon with toast plus a big cup of coffee. I would be all over that, but the smell of food brings bile to mouth. I push the tray aside.

"What's wrong, sugar?" he asks.

I throw my legs to the side of the bed and stand up. The room begins to spin and I have to brace my hand against the wall to remain upright.

"My stomach feels queasy."

"Maybe it was the lasagna you ate last night." He watches me closely.

"Maybe." I let go of the wall and with baby steps, I manage to walk around the bed toward the bathroom.

Oliver moves to my side and places a hand on my lower back. "You look ghastly. Are you going to throw up?"

"Jeez, thanks, babe. No, I'm not going to hurl. I just need a shower."

Oliver gives me an impish smile. "Want some company?"

I give him a droll look. "You just told me I look ghastly."

"Sugar, you know I would want you even if you were covered in blisters."

I give him a light shove. "Yew. Thanks for the visual. I think I'll manage showering on my own right now."

He laughs and walks back to the bed to retrieve the forgotten breakfast tray. "I'll bring this back to the kitchen and make you some tea."

"Don't throw my coffee away!"

Oliver widens his eyes. "I wouldn't dream of it."

When I called Derek last week, one thing he insisted I do, was to call my mother and tell her what was going on. He knows why we don't speak much these days, but he said I needed a family member with me at the appointment. It would be good to show Dr. Laurent I have a support system. I would rather have Karen with me, but I don't voice that out loud.

So here I am, on my way to Littleton to speak with my mother. When I called her yesterday, so last minute, I was hoping she wouldn't be around. But it turns out, today is her day off. The first thing that catches my attention when I park the brand new Range Rover Oliver gave me to replace the wrecked one, is the for sale sign in front of my old home. That ignites a myriad of feelings in me. I'm glad that Mom is finally ready to move on, but I'm also mad it took her so long. It's awful that one bad memory is able to trump all the good ones we made in that house. But that's how life is. Awful things have the tendency to cling to you much longer than they should no matter how hard you try to break free.

Mom is expecting me in the kitchen, the place where we used to hang out to talk about our day. She's sitting in her usual spot at the faded blue kitchen table with a mug of coffee in front of her.

"I just brewed some," she says as a way of greeting.

I walk to the cupboard and grab a cup, filling it to the brim. I can never have too much caffeine. I sit across from Mom, but I don't make eye contact, choosing to sip my drink instead. After a moment of silence on my part, she starts, "I listened to your song the other day on the radio, the duet. It's beautiful."

"Thanks. Yeah, the band is doing alright."

Mom frowns. "I'd say you're doing more than alright. So, are you still together with the good looking blond, the famous singer?"

"Yup. We live together now."

"Oh." I notice the sudden change in her demeanor, an underlying hurt. She's upset that I didn't tell her about moving in with Oliver.

"Mom, I'm not here to talk about my relationship or the band."

"Is it your father? Is he bothering you?"

I shake my head. I can't tell Mom that I suspect Daddy Dearest is trying to get rid of me. I don't know what she would do.

"No. It's about my health."

"Your health? Honey, you're scaring me. Are you sick?"

I nod. It's the only thing I'm capable of doing right now with the lump lodged inside my throat. Every time I think too long about this stupid clot and what it means, I get choked up.

"I discovered I have a blood clot in my brain. A residual of the attack most likely."

The color drains from my mother's face. "When did you find out?"

"A few months ago."

"A few months ago! And you're only telling me now?"

"I didn't want to tell anyone!" There are tears in my mother's eyes now and I feel my own eyes fill with them. "The doctor said I could have surgery, but I was too afraid to go through with it. So I didn't pursue it."

"You made that decision without telling me?"

"It was my decision to make. I don't want to fight with you about this. I'm here because I've reconsidered and I have an appointment with one of the best neurosurgeons in the country in a few hours. I would like you to come with me."

"Of course I'll come with you." Mom reaches out and grabs my hand, squeezing it lightly. "I'm sorry I haven't been the mother you deserve, Saylor. So very sorry."

"Me, too, Mom. Me, too. I want us to have a fresh start. I want you back in my life."

I didn't know that those words were the truth until I said them. I've missed my mother so much, but I pushed the feeling aside so I could go on living, so I could try to function.

"There's nothing in the world I want more." She stands up and walks around the table to give me a fierce hug. I hide my face against the flat of her stomach and let the tears run freely.

"I'm scared, Mom."

"Me, too. We'll get through this together. You won't have to be alone anymore."

I don't have the heart to tell her I was never alone. I had my friends, Liv's family, and now I have Oliver.

# CHAPTER 35

## OLIVER

pace back and forth in the backstage section of the Off-Summer Sessions Festival in Manhattan Beach. It's a newish music festival—it's only on its second year—but it has gathered a following already, with people coming all over the place for it.

"Where is she?" I turn to Allan.

"Relax, boss. She's stuck in traffic, she will be here."

I glance at the rest of the band. They are all present, ready for Wreck of the Day's concert. It's another televised performance. Saylor has yet to show her face. I glance at my phone and bring the browser screen up again. I don't fucking know why I keep staring at those blurry pictures of Saylor and Derek. They were taken earlier, in front of a big building I don't recognize. She's hugging him in some of them.

I grip the device tighter as jealousy runs freely through my veins. What the fuck is she doing with that arsehole again? I get alerted every time there's a new article online about the band, and this one came in an hour ago. The website where these pictures surfaced is a lesser-known gossip site, but I'm sure others will pick up the story soon. The headline is too juicy for them to pass up.

*Has Saylor Carter found a new beau? Does Oliver Best know? Wreck of the Day lead singer caught cheating on the British heartthrob.*

I didn't read the article itself, just scrolled down the page to see the pictures.

My brain knows Saylor is not cheating on me, but I can't help the feeling of betrayal just the same.

She arrives ten minutes before the band is supposed to go live, with her bodyguard in tow. Her make-up and hair are done, and she's wearing one of the outfits Monni selected for concerts. At least, she got that covered. We lock gazes and I don't hide my displeasure.

"I'm sorry," she says out of breath.

"Did you run here?" Remi chimes in before I have the chance to make a remark.

"Just from where the Uber driver dropped us off. It was a couple of blocks away. Traffic is insane."

"If you had arrived here on time, that wouldn't have been an issue," I say through clenched teeth.

"I already said I'm sorry. I had shit to do." She furrows her eyebrows and walks around me.

It's better if she stays away from me. I'm mad as hell and keeping my mouth shut until we're back home will be a fucking ordeal.

I watch as Tabatha gives Saylor hell for arriving so late. She's a little less subtle than me, gesturing wildly with her hands. Saylor takes the tongue lashing without saying a word, before she uses her phone to type a message. Tabatha looks at her own phone in turn and her angry expression changes significantly. She looks up again and says, "For real?"

Saylor nods and the band's bassist hugs her. What the fuck is going on? That little exchange is enough to snap the already stretched thin line that is my patience. I take a step toward the duo, but someone from the event announces it is time for the band to hop on stage. I grind my teeth and resign myself to wait until the concert is over. I'm expected to sing the duet with

Saylor half way through the show and I should get my head straight. One thing is sure, there won't be an impromptu kiss on stage tonight.

♡ ♡ ♡

## SAYLOR

I had to tell Tabatha about the doctor's appointment otherwise she would chew my head off. I couldn't let her go up on stage thinking I didn't care about the band. Oliver, unfortunately, will have to wait until we get home.

Despite knowing it won't be an easy conversation, my heart feels ten times lighter. Derek's mentor, Dr. Laurent, broke down every argument I had against surgery. He's confident he can perform a successful procedure with minimum invasion. His confidence and kind manner were key to setting my mind at rest.

I ignore the queasiness in my belly as I take my place in front of the mic. It's just pre-concert jitters. I'm taken aback by the wild roar from the audience when I greet them. I dreamed thousands times about this moment, but I couldn't have imagined what it would feel like to be up on stage, to be on the receiving end of such high voltage energy. There are catcalls and whistles, and I even spot in the crowd a fan made sign that reads, "Forget the boy band dude. Marry me, Blue."

I giggle and glance to the side of the stage, where Oliver is. His jaw is locked tight and he has his arms crossed in front of his chest. My smile fades. I can't believe he's that mad because I was late.

We start the show, singing the first single we released. Oliver will come up after the fourth song for our duet.

It's when I'm half way through the third song that my vision turns blurry and everything begins to spin. I mess up a bridge in my guitar solo but I don't think the audience noticed. I know Tabatha did because she leaves her designated spot on the stage and walks to me. She tries to pretend it's all part of the show, but I can read concern in her gaze. I force a smile, even though there are dark spots in my vision.

I manage to finish the song without any more slip ups, but I turn and signal to the band that I need a minute. We have scheduled pauses during our performance, but not until much later. I walk to where Sticks is behind her drums and grab one of the bottled waters that are tucked away, hidden from view. My hands are shaking and I can't open the cap.

I feel Tabatha's hand on my shoulder. "Blue, what's the matter?"

I put the heel of my hand against my forehead. "It's a dizzy spell. It will pass."

"Do we need to stop?"

I'm about to say no, when I feel my consciousness slipping away. I'm able to grab Tabatha's arm right before I fall into darkness.

# CHAPTER 36
## SAYLOR

don't know how long I was out for. When I come to, I'm on the backseat of a moving car and confused as hell. I can't concentrate on anything. My vision is hazy at best. It's only when I feel the soft brush of fingers against my cheek that my eyes are able to focus. Oliver's worried face is in my line of vision. His jaw is set hard and his eyes have a panicked glint in them that makes my heart fold in on itself. The pressure on my chest is too much to ignore, but I can't give into the urge to cry. Not right now. That time will come, sooner than I anticipated it seems.

"Where are you taking me?" I ask.

"Where do you think? To the bloody hospital of course."

"Ollie, I'm fine." I try to sit up, but Oliver's arm over my middle keeps me firm on the horizontal.

"Don't tell me you're *fine*. You fainted in the middle of the concert."

"Oh my God. Was the crowd mad?"

"Fuck the crowd. Sugar, you scared me to death."

I close my eyes for a moment and rub the spot between my eyebrows. "What a fiasco."

"Don't worry about that right now. Allan will take care of everything."

"Please take me home, Ollie. I don't need to go to the hospital."

He opens his mouth to argue but I interrupt him before he can, "I don't want to deal with the media right now."

I can practically see the wheels in his head turning as a myriad of conflicting emotions flash in his eyes. In the end, I win and he tells the driver to take us home. Once there, Oliver helps me up the stairs. Not that I can't walk on my own, but I need his touch right now, before I drop the truth bomb on our relationship. My heart is constricted in pain, gripped by fear. Knowing what I know about his past, I'm terrified of how he will react.

We head to our bedroom and I sit on the edge of the bed. Oliver begins to pace in front of me, his movements tense and jerky.

"You said you were one hundred percent well. Who's the fucking doctor who examined you? I want his head."

*Shit.* Derek. What am I going to do about him? I can't let him take the fall for my mess.

Sudden nausea hits me and I jump off the bed, making a beeline for the bathroom barely making in time. I hug the toilet bowl as I empty everything that is in my stomach. I'm dry heaving when I feel Oliver's presence behind me.

"Are you pregnant?"

His question comes out of nowhere and I'm too shocked to answer. It didn't sound like an angry accusation, though. Oliver takes my silence as affirmation. He drops his gaze to the floor and runs a hand through his hair.

"Fuck. Everything makes sense now. You're pregnant. That's what you told Tabatha earlier."

"Ollie…" I stand up on shaky legs.

He breaches the distance between us, grabbing my arms to hold me steady. "Sugar, why didn't you tell me?"

I'm overrun by a cowardice spell and pull back, walking to the sink to wash out my mouth.

"Did you think I would bail on you like your father bailed on your mother?"

I shake my head as I fight the tears that are already forming in my eyes. I splash my face with cold water for all the good that it does. I only manage to smear the heavy coat of mascara on my eyelashes. I reach for a tissue and clean the mess, a tactic to gain more time.

Oliver stops behind me and touches my shoulders. "Saylor. I *love* you. I never thought I would feel this way about anyone. *Ever*. You owned me the first moment I saw you."

Our gazes connect via the mirror's reflection and my heart overflows at the same time it breaks. How is it even possible? I turn so I can face him.

"Please, let me explain," I start to say, but Oliver talks over me.

"You don't have to worry. You won't have to go through this alone." He tucks a strand of my hair behind my ear and looks tenderly into my eyes. My heart shatters into a million pieces. And now I have to shatter his.

A lonely tear manages to escape one of my eyes and rolls down my cheek. Oliver kisses it away. "Don't cry, sugar."

"I'm not pregnant," I whisper.

He pulls back to stare at my face, frowning. "You aren't?" His tone of voice is disbelieving.

"Oliver, I'm dying." I force the words out before they get lodged in my throat.

He blinks a couple of times as if he can't quite comprehend what I'm saying. "What?"

"I have a blood clot in my brain."

There's a moment of unbearable silence as Oliver stares at me, frozen. It's worse than any shouting match we've had in the past. It's oppressive, it destroys me. His pale face turns ashen and he swallows hard. "When did you find out?"

I take a deep breath and stare at my feet. "A few months ago."

"A few months ago?" he says through clenched teeth. "Did you know that back in Hawaii?"

"Yes," I whisper and dare to raise my gaze again.

I thought I had seen Oliver broken before when I found him drowning his sorrows over the death of his brother. But it doesn't compare to the devastation I read in his eyes now.

"You should have told me. I deserved to know." He puts more distance between us as if he can't stand our proximity now.

"We weren't meant to last. We're supposed to be done after Hawaii."

"I love you!" He takes a step forward and stops suddenly. "I loved you then and I love you now. I deserved to know." He chokes up and brings a closed fist to his mouth before looking away. His entire frame is shaking.

I wipe the tears that are now streaming freely down my face. "I was afraid."

He whips his face back to mine. "Afraid of what?"

"That you wouldn't understand my decision."

"What decision?"

"I was told I could have surgery to remove the clot and I refused."

"You *refused?*"

Fury seems to crackle up his body. In a blur of movement, Oliver strikes the wall with his fist.

"Ollie!"

His hand is a bloody mess now, but he still pulls his arm back for another punch. I stop him before he can do more damage to himself. "Stop it!"

He looks at me with eyes that are brimming with unshed tears. "How could you do that?"

"I didn't want to risk turning into a vegetable. That would be worse than death."

"Who else knows?"

"Tabatha, my mother, Liv's mom, and Derek."

"Derek, of course." Oliver walks away from me.

"Before you go on another jealous rage, you have to know that Derek has helped me in more ways than one."

"That makes me feel so much better. You don't tell the man you claim to love about your self-imposed death sentence, but you tell your friend's ex? What the fuck, Saylor."

"I'm sorry! I messed up." I pull my hair back hard, ignoring the pain on my scalp. I deserve it. "I went to see Derek's mentor today, Dr. Laurent, a renowned neurosurgeon. I'm having the surgery, Ollie. I've changed my mind."

"All because of fucking Derek," Oliver says in a mocking tone.

I snap my face to his. "No, you idiot. Because of you. You are the reason I want to risk everything." I move closer and grab his chin, forcing Oliver to look into my eyes. "What I feel for you is bigger than anything, it reaches beyond the contours of my heart. You brought color to a world I didn't realize was gray before. I love you so damn much, Oliver. I don't want just a year with you. I want a whole life."

I can't believe I'm laying my heart out like this for Oliver to stomp all over it if he chooses. But I'm sick and tired of withholding the truth. I want him forever whether he's ready for it or not.

He captures my face between his hands and crushes his lips to mine for a kiss that is savage, almost cruel. He pushes me backwards until I hit the wall and he cages me in with his body. His hands leave my face to run down the sides of my body. His fingers brush the underside of my breasts before he cups them a little too roughly. I bite his lower lip in response, and suck it into my mouth while he teases my hard nipples.

He grunts right before he rips my top in two in an unrestrained move. I let out a yelp which Oliver promptly muffles with his tongue.

This won't be a sweet making love session. It will be hard

and punishing. This is where we both exorcise our demons. My fingers make quick work of his fly and his hard cock springs free only to be captured again by my hand. Still backed up against the wall, Oliver lifts me up, forcing me to let go of his erection. My legs wrap around his waist at the same time he tears the flimsy underwear I have on.

"Stop destroying my panties," I manage to say between kisses.

"Don't wear any and I won't." He glides inside of me in a swift move and I lose my ability to speak.

There's no going slow, Oliver pumps hard and fast and I squeeze tight around him, welcoming his fullness, loving the roughness. I dig my heels on his ass and Oliver responds with an assault of his own. He bites my shoulder and the pain sends me right over the edge. I scream his name and grip his arms tighter. Oliver's grunts turn more animalistic and before the waves of my orgasm subside, I feel his hot release inside of me. I come again, a less intense orgasm than before, but still enough to turn my body into mush. Oliver trembles in my arms and kisses the spot he has just bitten. I rest my cheek on his shoulder as I try to control my breathing.

Oliver chuckles next to my ear. "Back to back orgasms, sugar? I *am* a God."

I'm glad to hear some amusement in his tone, but I still feel the dark shadow hanging above our heads. I untangle my legs and drop to the floor. Maintaining my hold on his upper arms, I raise my eyes to meet his.

"Please say you forgive me."

His eyebrows furrow before his eyes soften. "I'm still fucking mad at you. I'm so mad I can't see straight."

I open my mouth but Oliver places a finger against my lips, silencing me.

"But how can I not forgive you? I will always forgive you, no matter how big you screw up. Don't you understand, Saylor? You own me. My body, my heart, my soul."

"You own me, too."

"Good." He smiles. "Now explain to me how Derek got involved in this story. Bear in mind I will never like the guy. That would be a betrayal of epic proportions to Bas."

I sigh loudly and let my shoulders drop, fixating my gaze on the hollow of Oliver's throat. "You might need a drink for that. You're not done getting angry at me."

# CHAPTER 37
## SAYLOR

t wasn't easy to convince Oliver to not say a word about Derek and the fake health report he signed for me. Granted, he only knows because I told him. He never opened the envelope, choosing to shove the document inside a drawer somewhere. I made him burn it. I couldn't risk that report ever surfacing to ruin Derek's life.

The truth didn't set me free, though. I won't ever feel that way until I get rid of the ticking time bomb in my head. But a huge weight has been lifted off my shoulders. After I told Oliver everything from the start, I realized there were no more secrets I was keeping from him. He holds my life in his hands now, he could ruin it if he wanted, but there's no doubt in my heart, no fear. I trust this man implicitly, blindly.

For once, I'm not filled with guilt when I wake in his arms the following morning. My head is resting on his chest and my legs are wrapped around his. I run lazy circles over his nipple and I smile when his skin breaks out in goose bumps. He hums with eyes still closed and holds me tighter. I let my hand trail down his torso until I find his bulging erection, making Oliver hiss. My fingers play with the head of his cock, spreading pre-cum around the sensitive skin with my thumb.

Without saying another word, Oliver rolls us over so he's now on top of me, between my legs. He kisses me right before he enters me, his cock sliding into my burning core with ease. He makes slow, circle movements with his hips each time he pumps into me, driving me insane in the best kind of way. I want him to go faster, but at the same time, I want to prolong the sweet agony.

When we come, almost simultaneously, I feel something click into my place inside my heart. There's a deeper connection between us now. I feel tethered to him in a way I wasn't before.

After we shower and get ready for the day, Oliver makes me breakfast. No one has showed up yet to end our time alone and for that I'm grateful. I'm nibbling on a crispy piece of bacon when Oliver finally broaches the subject we tried to forget for a few hours.

"When do you want to tell everyone?"

I swallow the food in my mouth before I reply. "I'll tell Remi, Sticks, and Allan today when they come in."

"Do you want me to invite Bas and Liv for dinner tonight?"

I stare at Oliver, startled. I don't know why I'm surprised he knows exactly what I need. "Yes."

"When is your next appointment?"

"Dr. Laurent ordered another CAT scan and a bunch of other exams. The CAT scan appointment is Monday. Would you—"

"I'll be there." He reaches out and squeezes my hand.

I look down at his hand covering mine and my stomach flips. "I'm so scared, Ollie." I bring my gaze up again. "What if something happens?"

"Then we will deal with it together."

I don't want to think about the worst case scenarios. I don't want to ask if he will still love me if I'm no longer me.

♡ ♡ ♡

We tell everybody when they show up at Renegades, a couple of hours later. Remi and Sticks are devastated, especially Remi who can't stop crying. Allan remains stoic and tries to look at things from the practical side. Do we issue a press release about my condition or not?

The media is already running wild with stories to explain my fainting. A lot of them allude to a potential pregnancy, but others hint at drug abuse as well. One particular article that does manage to get me rattled is the one that links me to the Senator. Someone has finally made the connection.

Within hours, other gossip sites catch wind of that rumor. The story is too juicy to pass up. So now I'm not only cheating on Oliver with Derek—he showed me the article last night—but I'm the illegitimate daughter of a Senator with a drug problem. Frigging fantastic.

When Liv calls to ask me how I am, I take the opportunity to invite her and Bas for dinner. By the cheery sound of her voice, she thinks Oliver and I have news. Maybe she's hoping we'll announce an engagement or something. If only that was the case. Not that I want to get married to Oliver. I don't need a wedding and a piece of paper to solidify my relationship with him. We already belong to each other.

I spend the rest of the day in the studio, working on some new songs. Music has always been able to heal my heart and I hope it will ease the anxiety and turmoil it still lingers there. I don't notice the passage of time nor when the girls leave. Oliver is the one who comes in to let me know Liv and Bas should be there at any moment. I put Rita back in her case and walk out the studio, feeling sudden jitters in my belly. I'm nervous about tonight, about what Liv will say.

# CHAPTER 38
## OLIVER

Saylor is fucking nervous. She's trying to hide it in front of our friends, but I know her too well. She wants to have dinner first before she tells Liv and Bas the news. I want to pull her tight against my chest and tell her everything will be okay, but I'm respecting her space. She doesn't want to be cuddled, she told me earlier.

We're having dinner outside by the pool. Saylor and Liv are chatting about mundane things. I'm by the outdoor bar, preparing drinks while Bas sits on the high stool opposite me. I'm glad Charlotte has decided to visit some friends in New York for a few days and is not around for the drama.

"Come on, mate. What's the reason for this impromptu dinner? Liv and I have a bet going on."

I raise an eyebrow at him and smirk. "Oh, really?"

"She thinks Saylor is pregnant, but I told her you're acting way too calm."

"What's that supposed to mean?"

"Dude, if you have knocked Saylor up, you would have gone mental. You hate kids."

I shake my head and think how I wish Saylor was pregnant.

"Nah, having a kid with her wouldn't be so bad."

I watch in amusement as my friend's jaw drops and his eyes widen. "She's fucking pregnant."

I shake the cocktail tumbler before I pour the girls' martinis into the glasses. "Bas, would I be making Saylor a dirty martini if she were pregnant?"

"I suppose not. You might be irresponsible, but she's not."

"Jeez, thanks."

Bas looks over his shoulder and stares at his wife for a moment before turning to me again. "Are you keeping tabs on all the gossip about Saylor? It's getting ugly, Ollie. Liv is very upset."

I take a deep breath and grind my teeth. "Yes. I'm trying to keep the worst of it from Saylor."

"There was a particularly nasty one penned by Craig Hawthorne."

I stop what I'm doing and almost let the tumbler slip from my hand. "Which one?"

"Shit. I thought you had seen it."

Bas pulls up his phone and shows me the article in question. I read it quickly and my blood is boiling when I reach the end of it. It's disgusting and filled with lies. They all make Saylor sound like a dirty whore, it takes slut-shaming to a whole new level.

"He's doing that to get to you," Bas says.

"I know and he will regret it."

"Ollie, don't do anything stupid."

My nostrils flare as I try to contain the fury running rampant through my veins. "Craig Hawthorne is scum and he just messed with the wrong person. He won't get away with this smear campaign against Saylor."

I don't know yet what I'm going to do about him, but by the time I'm done, he will be lucky if he can get a job writing copy for a local grocery store.

♡ ♡ ♡

## SAYLOR

Oliver is acting strange after the conversation he had with Bas and I wonder what they talked about. But that is a worry that I have push to the side. Dinner and dessert have come and gone, and now it's time for me to come clean.

"You must be wondering why I invited you guys to dinner with such short notice, especially after what happened yesterday."

"Yes. I'm dying to know, but you've been so secretive." Liv smiles at me.

"Well, I wanted us to have a good meal first before I drop the bomb."

Liv and Bas frown and stare at each other. I glance at Oliver, hoping his gaze will give me courage. He smiles and nods at me before mouthing 'You got this.'

"Blue, you're beginning to scare me. What's going on?"

I take a deep breath and tell my dearest friends everything. It has to come out all in one big whoosh before I lose my courage. When I'm done, there's a heavy silence all around us. Liv and Bas are staring at me like they've never seen me before. Suddenly, Liv jumps off her chair, walks around the table, and hugs me. Bas soon follows suit and together, they make a human sandwich out of me. When they step away and let me breathe, there are tears in their eyes.

"You're not mad at me?" I ask.

"How can I be? You've kept the truth from us to give us an untarnished wedding. I just wish you'd told us sooner."

"But I only changed my mind about the surgery a couple of days ago."

"You did, though. That's what matters. Now, the story would have been a whole lot different if you were still insisting on dying on us."

Oliver snorts next to me. "Like I would have let that happen."

A few weeks ago I would have said it wasn't his decision to make, but the fact he would fight for me, spreads warmth over my chest.

"Do you want to tell my folks or should I tell them?" Liv asks.

"Your mother already knows. I told her when I freaked out at the Thanksgiving dinner."

"Oh, Saylor…"

"What are the next steps?" Bas looks at me first, and then at Oliver.

"After Dr. Laurent gets the results of the exams he ordered, he wants to schedule the surgery as soon as possible."

"What about the commitments Wreck of the Day has? Not that you should worry about it, Blue, but you've worked so hard to get here," Liv says.

I look down at my lap, the guilt of letting Tabatha and the girls down seeping into my heart.

"Allan will handle that. The most important thing is getting Saylor well." Oliver grabs my hand and brings it to his lips to kiss my knuckles. His gesture eases the knot of anxiety in my belly. I smile at him.

From the corner of my eye, I see Bas wrap his arm around Liv's shoulder and kiss the side of her head while she stares at Oliver and me like a proud parent.

"Alright, alright. There's too much mushy stuff going on right now," I say. "I feel like I'm stuck in a Hallmark movie. It's time for some tequila."

# CHAPTER 39
## SAYLOR

For the next few days, everyone keeps walking on eggshells around me, as if they are afraid to do something that will upset me. I've lost count of how many times I entered a room and the conversation ceased. Oliver also forbade me to search my name online. He didn't want to upset me. I didn't Google myself because I chose not to, not because he ordered it, and I made sure to tell him that.

Today I feel cagey, on edge. My nerves are fried and I'm sick and tired of the kid glove treatment. It's time for me to stop hiding and face the real world. So the first thing I do when I'm alone is power up my laptop and bring up the browser on my screen. First, I search for Wreck of the Day and I'm glad that not all top links refer to the fiasco performance at the beach. It's when I Google my name that the nasty comes out. I click on a random link and I'm horrified to see pictures of me when I was out clubbing with my friends. They all make me look like a drunk whore. Bile pools in my mouth and my vision turns blurry. I clench my jaw and read the entire piece of garbage. The last paragraph is what delivers the final twist of the blade. It alludes to my involvement in a murder case. How in the world had they come by that information? I was a minor, my name should have never have leaked to the press. What if they keep digging and find out the truth?

"Sugar?"

I turn to find Oliver right behind me. I didn't even hear him enter the room.

"Ah, luv. I asked you not search your name."

"Did you see this?" I push the laptop toward him.

He picks it up and frowns. "No. This must be a new one."

"They mention the attack."

Oliver's gaze connects with mine. He knows what that could mean. He focuses again on the screen, his expression serious and determined. "I'll get to the bottom of this."

"How? What can you do?"

He shuts the laptop off and puts it away. "I don't want you to read any more of this garbage. You can't get upset."

"Stop treating me like I'm a china doll! I'm not breakable."

My outburst seems to startle him. His expression softens. He walks back to where I am and kneels in front of me. "But you *are* breakable. I don't want to make your condition worse."

I want to refute him, but my body betrays me and undermines any argument I might have. I sway on the spot and I have to close my eyes to make the room stop spinning. I feel Oliver's hands on my arms, steadying me.

"You're taking the day off today."

"I'm fine."

"No, you're not. I'm heading out. I'll put Charlotte on watch duty."

"I'm sure she'll love that."

I let Oliver guide me back to bed and when my head hits the pillow, sudden exhaustion hits me. Oliver kisses my forehead and says he will be back after lunch. I don't even see him leave, falling asleep almost instantly.

♡ ♡ ♡

## OLIVER

It doesn't take long for me to find out where Craig Hawthorne works. All it took were a few phone calls to get the name of the trashy magazine that employs that piece of scum. I head to their office, not knowing what I will do if that weasel is there. The receptionist, a ditzy blonde with more stuffing in her lips than a turkey, is quick to say Craig has gone out to lunch and tells me where he likes to eat. She recognized me as soon as she laid her eyes on me. I wasn't trying to hide my identity.

I turn on my heel before she has the chance to ask for a stupid selfie with me, or an autograph. The magazine's building is in downtown L.A. and the restaurant Craig prefers is within walking distance. I stride with purpose, practically shoving people out of my way. The closer I get to the place, the angrier I become. Saylor's tear-streaked and panicked face comes to mind and I curl my hands into fists.

I enter the busy restaurant and ignore the hostess. It takes me a few minutes to find the rat eating at a table in the middle of the establishment. My gaze shifts to his companion and things become crystal fucking clear to me. Sitting opposite Craig is Saylor's half sister, the woman I met at the charity ball a few months back. The Senator has been using his own daughter to supply info to Craig. I don't know who I want to hurt more, Craig or him.

I make a beeline in the duo's direction and they only notice my presence when I stop in front of their table.

"Fancy seeing you here, Craig," I say.

The man looks at me with a glint of surprise in his dark eyes. "What are you doing here?"

"I came to have a little chat with you, but I see you have company." I shift my gaze to Saylor's sister. The woman has the decency to look guilty at least.

"I'd better leave." She folds her napkin and places it on top of her uneaten salad.

"Why leave? Let's a have party shall we? I would love to know what you, the daughter of a prestigious Senator, have in common with this piece of shit here."

"You'd better watch your tongue, boy."

"Or what? What are you going to do, rat?"

The perfectly coiffed woman stands up. "I don't need this."

She walks away and I follow her. I can deal with Craig later. When she clears the tables section, I grab her forearm and steer her into the restroom's direction.

"Hey! What do you think you're doing?"

"I need to talk to you."

"I don't care. Let me go." She tries to pull her arm free, but I hold tighter.

"No. I'm going out on a limb here you don't want to cause a commotion. What would Daddy Dearest say?"

She shuts her mouth and lets me drag her to the less visible part of the restaurant. There's an alcove between the men's and ladies' room and it's where I stop, letting go of her arm finally.

"That was uncalled for." She rubs the sore spot.

"I don't think so. What the fuck is your end game here? Weren't the threatening notes and murder attempt not enough for your father? He has to drag her name through the mud as well?"

Saylor's sister holds her hand up. "Stop. What are you talking about? Notes and a murder attempt?"

"Don't play stupid with me. I know very well your father is behind all that. I just want you to give him a message from me. If something happens to Saylor, I will destroy him. If he has done his homework, he knows who I am, he knows I have the means. If Saylor dies because of your family's bullshit, I will go after every single one of you."

I walk away before the woman has the chance to spill any lies. When I return to the main area, I notice Craig is no longer there. Of course, the coward has run away.

*I will destroy you too, rat.*

# CHAPTER 40
## SAYLOR

When Oliver returns, he won't tell me where he's been or what he's done. He only says I don't need to worry about anything, the gossip about my attack will stop. He spends the next hour locked inside Charlotte's room, doing God knows what. I hate being left out, but I can't fault anyone but myself. I've let Oliver and the girls keep me in a bubble, sheltered. I acted like a coward again and I'm done being the damsel in distress.

I'm feeling much better after my weird morning nap. My face still has a sickly color, so I apply a heavy coat of make-up. I do my hair next which resembled a bird's nest before. When it's nice and shiny again, I go in search of my favorite kickass, take no prisoners outfit, my racer back skull shirt and my skin tight, ripped jeans which I pair with the famous fuck-me-heels Oliver loves so much. I stare at my reflection in the mirror and for the first time in days, I feel like my old self again.

I stride out the gloomy bedroom toward the main space of the house. There I find exactly the person I was looking for, Allan.

He senses my approach and looks up from his computer. His

gaze drops to my shoes and then slowly goes back up as he takes me in.

"You look better."

"Thanks. I feel better." I grab a chair and push it toward Allan, sitting opposite him with his desk between us. "I want to issue a statement about my condition."

He leans back in his seat and watches me with a scrutinizing gaze. "That would be the best course of action, but have you talked to Oliver about it?"

"There's nothing to discuss. Dr. Laurent wants to perform the surgery as soon as possible. That will mean any future commitments Wreck of the Day has made will have to be cancelled or postponed."

"Yes. I know." Allan rubs his face and seems worried.

"Is that going to screw up the future of the band?"

He shakes his head. "Your duet with Oliver is still high up in the charts and you're still part of the teen movie's soundtrack. I'm wondering what we should do about the rumors involving your biological father. There has been a lot of speculation about it. A statement should have come from his office, but it hasn't happened yet."

"I signed a contract abdicating of all my rights. I don't think I can say anything without creating a bunch of legal trouble for me."

Allan nods and seems lost in thought. After a moment, he goes back to his computer and begins to type away. "I'll focus on your press release about your upcoming surgery then. I'll let you read it before I send it to the press."

"Thanks, Allan. I appreciate it."

I stand up and decide to spend some time by the pool. There I find Charlotte in a two-piece bikini, working on her already fabulous tan. I wonder where she gets her golden olive skin from. Oliver is pasty white like most Britons I know.

I sit on the chaise lounge next to hers and she turns her face my way. "Why are you wearing all those clothes? You'll get awful looking tan lines."

"I didn't realize it was so hot today."

"Yes, you've been cooped up inside for too long. I hope you are feeling better."

"I am."

"I'm sorry about the shit storm that has hit the tabloids. How are you holding up?"

I shrug. "It's harder in the beginning, you know? But now, I don't care. Let them spew their lies. I guess I'm growing a thicker skin."

"Gossip bloody sucks."

"So, how is everything with school?"

"Brilliant. I start next semester. I can't wait. I need to find my own place, of course. This house is too crowded."

"Yes."

Charlotte sits up and pulls her sunglasses up her head. "You don't mind? Having Allan and your friends here all the time privy to your life with Oliver? That would drive me insane."

"Honestly, I haven't had much time to dwell on it. Sure, it would be nice if Renegades Headquarters wasn't here."

"I haven't had a chance to talk to you alone, but I just want to let you know I'm fucking ecstatic that you and my brother have worked things out. I've never seen Oliver happier, despite everything."

I drop my gaze to my lap. "He makes me happy, too. I just hope…"

"Hey, your surgery will go fine. Don't stress about it."

I glance at her face and smirk. "It's a bit hard not to stress about it. They're going to cut my head open."

"I know, so *Grey's Anatomy*. Is Dr. Laurent as hot as McDreamy?"

A snort escapes my lips. "Not quite. For starters, he's over sixty."

Charlotte wrinkles her nose. "Yew. How about your friend?

Derek is his name, right? By the way Oliver gets mad jealous every time the guy is mentioned, I have to assume he's hot."

I smile. "Yes. Derek is easy on the eyes."

"McDreamy or McSteamy?" Charlotte leans forward.

"Hum. I'd say McSteamy on looks, McDreamy in personality."

Charlotte lets herself fall backwards on the chaise lounge. "Swoon. I have to meet him. He sounds like the perfect boyfriend material."

"Sure. I can make that happen. But I don't think Oliver will like that idea very much."

Charlotte gives me an impish grin, very similar to the one her brother has mastered. "That's what makes it even more appealing."

# CHAPTER 41
## SAYLOR

## A WEEK LATER

The outpour of support and positive messages that came after Allan put out the press release about my health condition was overwhelming and unexpected. The terrible rumors stopped like magic including the one that guessed I was the illegitimate daughter of Senator Holloway. The man himself never addressed those rumors. Good. I don't ever want anyone to know about my genetic connection to him.

Tomorrow is the day my fate will be decided. After Dr. Laurent reviewed the results of all my exams, he scheduled the surgery. I'm expected to check into the hospital early in the morning.

I saw my closest friends yesterday. Oliver organized a little get together with Liv's help and they all came—including Emma and Ken—to wish me good luck and spend quality time with me. Even after a successful surgery, the road to recovery won't be easy. It was a bittersweet occasion. There were times I caught my friends looking at me funny, but no one ever mentioned the fact that maybe last night would be the last time they'd see me.

I try not to dwell in pessimistic thoughts. They come unbidden sometimes and my heart is seized by uncontrollable fear when it happens. I don't say anything, especially not to Oliver. I know he has those moments too, even if he tries to hide them from me.

Oliver wasn't in bed when I woke up this morning. Instead, I found a note from him and a single red rose. The note tells me to get into the shower and wear the dress he left draped over the chair in our room. My gaze travels to one of the corners where the piece of furniture is, and sure enough, there's a red dress folded on it. I wonder what Oliver is up to. He has been more closed off than usual for the past few days and I just assumed it was his way to deal with my impending surgery.

I do as the note says and get ready. When I venture out of the bedroom, I find the house deserted. It's so weird to not hear a sound. I've grown used to the hectic, full house dynamic of Renegades HQ. I find another note and a single red rose on the kitchen counter. I bring the flower to my nose before I read the card next to it. Oliver says to hop into the car that is waiting for me outside the house.

Curiouser and curiouser.

The door bell rings and I wonder if that's my ride. I grab my purse and practically skip down the flight of stairs. When I open the door, I almost have to do a double take. My half sister, Vanessa Holloway, is standing there, wearing a Chanel suit and big sunglasses.

I cross my arms in front of my chest and glare at her. "What are you doing here?"

"Hello, Saylor. Do you mind if I come in?"

I should just shut the door in her face, but I'm too curious to do that. This is the first time anyone from my father's side of the family has reached out to me in person.

"I have to be somewhere, so this better be quick." I move out of the way so she can pass.

"I promise not to take up too much of your time."

I let her take the stairs first because I'm leery to give my back to her. She reaches the landing and removes her sunglasses, doing a quick scan of the room before turning to me.

"Are you alone in the house?"

"Yes. But I have a chauffeur waiting for me outside. If I don't come out soon, he'll know something is up."

Her eyebrows shoot up to the heavens. "Do you think I came here to kill you?"

"I don't know. Your father sure as hell tried."

She lets out a loud sigh. "I know nothing about my father's dealings. Oliver mentioned the threatening notes. I swear I have nothing to do with it."

"Wait? When did you and Oliver speak?"

"A few weeks back. I was having lunch with an old acquaintance of his."

Oliver never mentioned anything me and I feel betrayed as hell. I try to hide my emotions. I don't want to give Vanessa the upper hand.

"He's very protective of you," she continues.

"Yes. He is."

"Anyway, I came here to apologize."

I raise an eyebrow at her. That's the last thing I was expecting to hear from the woman. "Explain."

She looks away and begins to walk the room. "My father and I don't get along. He is a difficult man. You're lucky he doesn't want anything to do with you."

I snort and Vanessa looks at me again. "I envy you, your freedom. You don't know how much it kills me to admit that, especially to you."

"Wow, thanks a lot. If you came here to apologize for being jealous of me, you shouldn't have bothered. I don't give a rat's ass about your feelings. The fact we share DNA means to nothing to me."

"I'm the one who leaked to the press you are the Senator's illegitimate daughter."

"Why?" Shit, Vanessa is full of surprises.

"Because I wanted to hurt him."

I cross my arms in front of my chest. "Were you also responsible for all the other nasty rumors about me?"

She shakes her head. "No, that was Craig's doing. He has a vendetta against your boyfriend. I didn't realize that until I was in too deep and for that I'm truly sorry. I wasn't thinking about what my actions would mean to you. I only wanted to get back at my father."

"What did he do to you?"

Vanessa lets out a humorless laugh. "The question is what *didn't* he do to me."

I sense there's a lot Vanessa is not telling me, but I honestly don't care to know. I can't summon an ounce of sympathy for her. She's only here because I might die tomorrow and she wants to unburden her guilty conscience.

"That's it?"

"Yes. That's it."

"Alright. You can leave now."

"I hope everything goes well for you tomorrow. I'd say I'd pray for you if I believed in any of that."

She walks past me and I follow her closely. I want to make sure she's out of my house. I shut the door as soon as she's out, and I lean against it, taking deep breaths. Her visit affected me more than I expected. I need time to recover.

I feel my phone vibrate in my purse, and when I fish it out, I see Oliver's text message. 'Where are you?'

*Shit*. I forgot about him. I open the door once more, and make sure there's no sign of Vanessa before venturing out onto the curb. Tony gets out of the car and opens the door for me.

"Hi, Tony. Sorry to keep you waiting."

"No problem, Saylor."

"Where are we going?" I ask before I slide in.

"I'm not at liberty to say."

Of course he isn't. I finally enter the vehicle and Tony closes the door. Once inside the warm interior, I spot on the black leather seat another red rose but no note this time. I try to put Vanessa's visit aside and the fact that Oliver spoke to her and didn't tell me. I don't want to fight with him, especially about her.

I stare out the window during the entire drive, but I can't for the life of me guess where Tony is taking me. Our final destination turns out to be a private airport. He stops at the gate briefly. Security check happens in the blink of an eye. Tony drives all the way to the tarmac, parking close to a small plane. He once again opens the door for me, and I have to hold onto the skirt of my knee length dress so I won't pull a Marilyn Monroe move. Controlling my hair against the wind proves a little bit more difficult. It dances wildly, getting in my line of vision. I finally manage to grab a handful and see that Oliver is waiting for me in front of the plane, holding another single rose. He's dressed smartly as well, with dark pants, a button down shirt, and a jacket. His eyes are hidden behind the sunglasses, but I can feel his appreciative stare just the same.

I put more swing into my hips as I walk in his direction, stopping right in front of him.

"What's all this?"

"I wanted to take you out to dinner."

"And we need a plane to get there?"

"The restaurant I have in mind is in another state."

"You're crazy. I have to be at the hospital early tomorrow morning."

"I know. We'll make it back in time." He takes my hand and brings it to his lips for a kiss.

"Where are we going?"

Oliver takes his sunglasses off and seems nervous all of the sudden. "Well, that depends on your answer, sugar."

Still holding my hand, Oliver reaches inside his jacket pocket with the free one. A second later, he pulls out a sparkly diamond ring from it. I stop breathing and stare at the piece of jewelry for a few seconds without blinking. Then my gaze connects with his again.

"I don't know what will happen tomorrow and I've gone crazy obsessing about it. But the one thing I know, the one thing is crystal clear, is that I want you to be with me forever. I want you to go into that operating room knowing I will never abandon you, no matter what happens. My heart will always beat for you, Saylor. It will always belong to you."

"Ollie…"

"I want you to be my wife, sugar. Please say yes."

I let go of his hand and ignore the offered ring only to grab Oliver's face and kiss him. His arm snakes around my waist and pulls me closer while his tongue matches the tempo of my frenetic kiss beat by beat. He leans back just a fraction and asks in a husky voice, "Does this mean it's a yes?"

"Of course it's a yes."

We kiss again and I ignore the wind dancing between my legs, blowing the light fabric of my dress in all directions. I might be giving Tony a hell of a view, but I don't care. Oliver finally manages to break us apart to put the ring on my finger. It fits perfectly. I stare at the rock, and I'm mesmerized by the prism of colors the diamond produces when it catches the light.

"So, where are we going?" I ask.

"What do you think? Vegas of course."

♡ ♡ ♡

We get married in a cheesy Elvis themed chapel. On the way there, Oliver asked me if I was upset I wasn't getting a big wedding. I never cared for any of that stuff, so I put his mind at ease. Liv will be the one upset she didn't get to plan the party. After the ceremony, we checked-in at the Venetian hotel to officially consummate our marriage before we headed back to L.A. Oliver may or may not have taken me to O-town on the flight back as well.

When we get home, it's past two in the morning and I'm exhausted. We have to be up again in a few hours, and although I'm sure Dr. Laurent would frown upon the fact that I didn't get enough rest, I wouldn't have slept much if I had gone to bed at a decent hour anyway.

Liv and Sebastian come to see me at the hospital before I begin to prep for surgery. There's a moment of tension because Derek has also stopped by to say hello. He doesn't linger, knowing how his presence is not entirely welcome.

I haven't told anyone yet that Oliver and I eloped, and I removed my ring before coming here. I'm filling out paperwork when my mother asks the nurse if she needs to sign anything as well. The nurse looks down at the form in her hand and frowns.

"No, ma'am. Your daughter is married. Her husband already signed the required forms."

You could hear a pin drop within the silence that takes over the room.

"Her husband?" Mom looks at me confused.

"Uh…"

"No way! You and Oliver got married?" Liv asks.

Oliver comes into the room then, holding a cup of coffee I'm not allowed to drink anymore.

"Sugar, I thought we were going to tell them together."

"You got married without telling me?" Mom sounds so upset.

"It was a spur of the moment decision," I say lamely.

Bas goes to Oliver to do the hug, slap on the back thing. "Congrats, mate. Welcome to the club."

"Thanks." He smiles in my direction and my heart soars.

Liv crosses her arms and pouts. "I can't believe you didn't invite us."

"Aw, babe. Are you mad you didn't get to plan Blue's

wedding?" Bas wraps his arm around her shoulder, pulling her closer to him.

"Yes."

"You can throw me a post surgery party," I say.

Dr. Laurent comes into the room and announces that we need to begin to prep for surgery. He brings the anesthetist with him and asks that only immediate family remains. Suddenly, things become too real and my stomach ties into knots. Both doctors do the best that they can to make me relax, but it's impossible. When they are done, I ask for a few minutes alone with Oliver. Mom gives me a long glance but she doesn't object.

Once everyone is out, Oliver takes a seat next to my bed and holds my hand. "What is it, sugar?"

"I want you to promise me something."

He must sense he's not going to like what I'm about to say. His shoulders tense as a deep V forms between his eyebrows.

"If something happens during surgery and I don't wake up, I want you to turn off the machines."

"Saylor, I can't do that."

"You must, Ollie. I don't want to live as a vegetable, hooked up to a machine. That's not living at all. If I go into a coma and don't wake up after a few months, I want you to let me go."

Oliver clenches his jaw and his face turns red. His eyes are bright and I know he's fighting tears that are threatening to spill.

"I'll love you forever." I touch his cheek.

He leans over and kisses me, tenderly after first, but then it changes, it becomes fierce, wild. It tastes like a goodbye kiss.

He pulls back and rests his head on my lap. "I'll love you forever and a day."

We both chuckle at his ill attempt at humor. I run my fingers through his hair. "Promise, Ollie. Please."

He raises his head and the look in his gaze is devastating, it shatters my heart into a million fragments.

"Anything you want, sugar. But I need you to promise me something as well."

"What is it?"

"Promise you will come back to me."

There are a thousand ways I can interpret his request, but I would abide to it in any way he meant.

"I promise."

# CHAPTER 42
## OLIVER



t has been three weeks since Saylor had the surgery and she's still hasn't woken up. Christmas and New Year's Eve came and went and I wouldn't know if it weren't for the decorations. These have been the worst weeks of my life.

In the initial days after the surgery, Dr. Laurent assured us the coma was normal. Saylor's brain needed time to recover. There were some complications during surgery and her brain had swollen up a bit. He was optimistic at the time, but now there's no denying things are not looking good. I remember the promise I made Saylor, that I would let her go if she didn't wake up after a few months, but I don't think I will be strong enough to do it. I can't bear the thought of going on with my life without her in it.

After a disheartening conversation with the good old doc, I find myself doing something I've never done before. I head to the hospital's chapel. The arched doors are wide open, but I don't enter the peaceful room right away. Instead, I stare at the cross above the altar, feeling lost. I'm not sure if I remember how to pray. There's no one around and when I finally find the courage to enter the space, my steps echo, disturbing the silence in the room. The air is cooler here, so I pull my jacket closer together before I kneel on the pew. I rest my elbows against the back crest of the row in front of me and hide my face between my hands. All this time, I've been trying to remain calm and positive. I didn't succumb to my old vices because I don't want Saylor to wake up to a mess.

I can't hold the swell of emotions brewing in my chest any longer and I let it all out an anguished sob. My entire body trembles as I'm taken over by darkness and despair.

I don't notice that I'm no longer alone before someone touches my shoulder. I look up and find Bas standing there. I wipe my damp face with the back of my forearm, not feeling an ounce of shame my best mate caught me in this pathetic state. It's not the first time he has seen me at my worst.

"Were you just praying?"

"If you call crying like a banshee praying, then yes." I stand up and hear my knees crack. Jesus, how long have I been here?

"You must have put out a hell of a show. Saylor is awake."

My heart stops for a second before it takes off at the speed of an F1 race car. "Why didn't you tell me sooner?"

I stride out the chapel and break into a run in the hallway. When I get to Saylor's room, her mother and Liv are huddled together in a corner, trying not to be in the way of Dr. Laurent who is currently checking Saylor's eyes. They raised her bed to a sitting position, but she still has tubes everywhere. It doesn't matter, her eyes are open.

The doctor asks her a bunch of mundane questions and she answers most of them with only a hint of confusion. The man finally notices me hovering by the door and calls me in. Saylor turns her face in my direction and just being able to see the color of her eyes again almost makes the cry fest resume.

Her delicate eyebrows furrow before she glances at Liv. "Who is he?"

I freeze as an invisible dagger strikes at my heart, twisting slowly as it goes in. The pain is so sharp, I can't draw air into my lungs. Just a simple three-word question and I'm left hollow. She doesn't know who I am.

"Blue, that's Oliver, you don't remember him?"

"No, should I?"

Liv trades a worried glance with Bas. Saylor catches her reaction and continues. "Why is Sebastian here, too? Did you make up?"

"Doc, what's going on?" I ask, unable to keep my mouth shut any longer.

"Saylor, what's the last thing you remember?"

"I don't know. Everything is such a mess. I guess I remember Liv's farewell party."

"Before I went to London?"

"Yes. I'm forgetting stuff aren't I?" Her gaze bounces around the room before she fixes her eyes on me again. "Are you my boyfriend or something?"

I open my mouth but no words come forth. This cannot be real.

Saylor's mom approaches the bed and squeezes her hand. "Darling, that man over there is your husband."

**TO BE CONTINUED**

♡ ♡ ♡

**Thank you for reading *Wreck of the Day*. Saylor and Oliver's story concludes in *Devils Don't Fly*.**
**AVAILABLE NOW!**

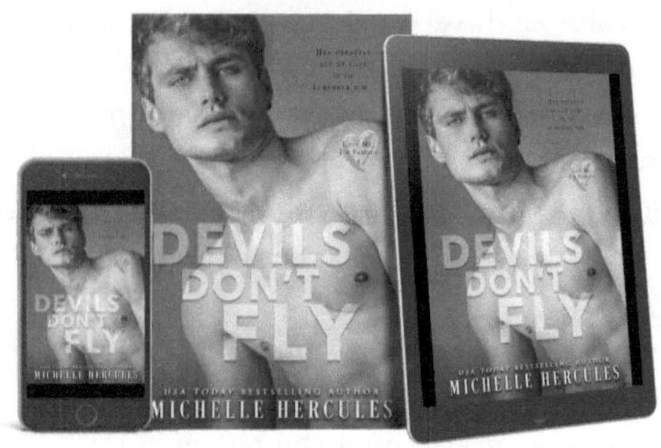

**Her greatest act of love is to remember him**

Have you ever wished to one day wake up and discover all your dreams have come true?

It happened to me and no, it wasn't the work of a fairy godmother.

My music is playing on the radio, my face is splattered on the cover of every magazine, and I can't remember how I got there. The cherry on top is discovering the most devilish handsome man I've ever met is—wait for it—my husband.

Of all my denied memories, Oliver Best is the hot enigma that confuses me the most. I can't fight the chemistry, the raw attraction between us. But the question lingers, can I fall in love with him again?

*This is the FINAL book in Saylor & Oliver's trilogy.

**ONE-CLICK TODAY!**

# FREE NOVEL

## CATCH YOU

Want to read another deliciously fun contemporary romance by Michelle Hercules? Then **CLICK HERE** to get your FREE copy of *Catch You*.

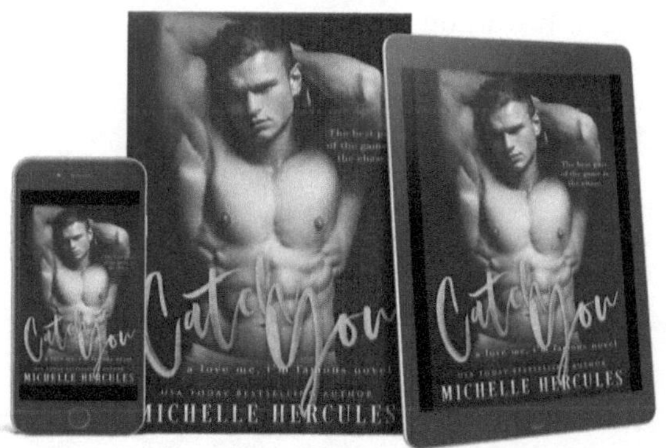

**Pride and Prejudice meets Veronica Mars in this enemy-to-lovers romance.**

KimberlyI had always thought Owen Whitfield fit the mold of

the brainless jock perfectly. Group of idiot friends? Check. Vapid girlfriend? Check. Ego bigger than the moon? Check. As long as he stayed out of my way, coexisting with his kind was doable. Until one day our worlds collided, changing everything. He pissed me off so badly that I had no choice but to give him a taste of his own medicine. Little did I know that my act of revenge would come back to bite me in the ass. How was I supposed to know Owen would turn out to be the best partner in crime I could hope for?

Owen never paid much attention to Kimberly Dawson, but I knew who she was. Ice Queen was what we called her. She was gorgeous, no one could deny that. But she was also a condescending bitch, which was enough reason for me to stay the hell away from her. She thought I was a dumb jock, and that was okay until she came crashing into my life. Against my better judgment, I let her embroil me in her shenanigans, forcing us to spend too much time together. It was my doom. She got under my skin. She was all I could think about. I never thought I would be the knight in shining armor to anyone, not until she came along.

**CLICK HERE to get your free copy!**

**OR**

**Scan the code!**

# ABOUT THE AUTHOR

*USA Today* Bestselling Author Michelle Hercules always knew creative arts were her calling but not in a million years did she think she would become an author. With a background in fashion design she thought she would follow that path. But one day, out of the blue, she had an idea for a book. One page turned into ten pages, ten pages turned into a hundred, and before she knew it, her first novel, The Prophecy of Arcadia, was born.

Michelle Hercules resides in Florida with her husband and daughter. She is currently working on the *Blueblood Vampires* series and the *Rebels of Rushmore* series.

**Join Michelle Hercules' Reader Group:**
https://www.facebook.com/groups/mhsoars

**Sign up for Michelle Hercules' Newsletter:**
https://mhsoars.activehosted.com/f/11

facebook.com/michelleherculesauthor
instagram.com/michelleherculesauthor
tiktok.com/@michelleherculesauthor
bookbub.com/authors/michelle-hercules
patreon.com/michellehercules